STAR DUST

FLY ME TO THE MOON
BOOK ONE

Emma Barry & Genevieve Turner

Publisher's Note: This is a work of fiction. Names, characters, places, and incidents are a product of the author's imagination. Locales and public names are sometimes used for atmospheric purposes. Any resemblance to actual people, living or dead, or to businesses, companies, events, institutions, or locales is completely coincidental.

Book Layout ©2013 BookDesignTemplates.com

Star Dust/ Emma Barry & Genevieve Turner. -- 1st ed.
ISBN 978-1544299310

That was the record Kit was aiming for. One that could never be broken.

"She's looking good," the mechanic said, wiping his hands on a rag. "You ought to think about leaving some of those altitude records for the other pilots to grab."

Fat chance of that. Aviators were the most competitive bastards out there. Always jockeying to see who flew the fastest, the highest, won the most dogfights. A test pilot didn't step aside for others to go first—he raced them all to *be* the first.

Kit was first—at the moment—and he meant to stay there.

"Let's get her ready," he said. "See how high we can go today." He had a good feeling, a sense that something momentous was about to be shattered.

He went to the locker room to put on his flight suit, clearing his mind of everything but his plane, the feel of the controls in his hand, the response of the X-15 to his motions—a flight like this required every bit of concentration.

He was reaching for his helmet, the oxygen tube snaking from it like an elephant's trunk, when Lieutenant Commander Reynolds burst in.

"They're calling muster." Reynolds didn't even enter the room, just hung on the doorframe, eyes wide.

PROLOGUE

Naval Air Station Patuxent River, Maryland
October 5, 1957

"Thinking about setting a new altitude record?" Lieutenant Commander Christopher Campbell—Kit to everyone who didn't call him Campbell—grinned as he unwrapped a stick of Juicy Fruit. "I was thinking about it," he told the mechanic.

He was more than thinking about it—he was going to do it.

Wind whipped through the hangar, plastered his clothes against his body for a moment, and then calmed again.

"How is she today?" he asked.

She was the X-15, a test plane designed to go as high as possible. More rocket than plane, really, with her long, cylindrical body and short stubby wings. She handled like a drunk pig, but she didn't need the grace of a dancer. She only needed to take him to the edge of the atmosphere, where the blue of the sky bled into the black of space.

If she took him fifty miles up, he'd be the first man in space.

To Richard. Everyone dreams of going to the moon, but
you made it happen—E.B.

For B, who doesn't even know he inspired this—G.T.

"Everything's grounded today." A little rushed, his words, but not really panicked.

Huh. Kit chewed his gum slowly. Something big must have happened.

"All right. I'm coming."

As Reynolds dashed off, Kit's heart began to pound. He peeled out of the flight suit, his hands steady, his skin cool even in humid Indian summer of Maryland.

When he reached the muster room, all of the Pax River test pilots had assembled, even the off-duty aviators.

Whatever it was, it was serious. Kit eased into a metal folding chair and glanced around, but there was nothing in the pilots' faces to suggest they knew what was happening either.

Captain Watson paced the front of the room. A radio next to him was transmitting an odd pulse—a strange kind of chirping, like a robotic canary, about three pulses per second.

What the hell was that?

Kit wasn't the only puzzled one, judging by the furrowed brows and pinched mouths, but the aviators' postures were loosely alert. Like Kit, most of them had flown in Korea—it took more than a general muster and a weird radio signal to rattle them.

No point getting excited until the enemy was sighted. And Kit didn't see one here.

Captain Watson paused and took a look around with his hands behind his back. "You've all been called here today because of that"—he gestured to the radio—"because of that noise."

They all waited for him to go on. Kit chewed his Juicy Fruit, the taste almost gone now. But he still kept working at it, if only to keep himself steady.

"It's an artificial satellite," the captain said. "Transmitting from an Earth orbit."

Every man in the room became a little more alert, a little brighter. An object orbiting Earth, a man-made thing touching space—the possibilities of it electrified all of them.

It looked like the Naval Research Facility had finally figured out how to keep their rockets from exploding on the pad. *Go Navy.*

"It's not ours," Captain Watson finished heavily.

Their eager anticipation turned into chilled anxiety.

"The Soviets beat us?" Reynolds asked, channeling the incredulity of every man in the room.

"Are we scrambling fighters?" another man asked.

Jesus, a Soviet satellite, hovering overhead… Who knew what it might do? The enemy *was* here, just miles above them.

"No." Captain Watson regained a touch of his composure. "The threat level is raised for the moment, but what can we do about a satellite? We can't shoot it down."

"Fuck," Kit muttered under his breath. He knew better than most how futile such a thing would be. He'd imagined heading fifty miles up today—and that satellite was probably a hundred and fifty miles up.

A satellite launched into space, and America wasn't the one who'd done it. What was next?

A man in orbit. That was next.

And then? Then the moon.

The Soviets could conquer space.

His jaw clenched tight, the Juicy Fruit clamped between his molars. He stared at the radio, chirping out that never-ending loop. It had been odd before he knew what it was, but now it was alien, unsettling. A warning that the Soviets had won.

At least this battle. There was still time to put a man in orbit. To put a man on the moon.

Kit had sworn to defend this country at home and abroad. The Soviets wanted to take this fight to space? Well, Kit was ready.

He'd been ready since he was a boy, really. Dreaming of the stars…

But this wasn't a time for dreams. It was time to act. America was up to the task. They'd beat the Soviets—and Kit would be part of that effort.

He wasn't sure how, but he would be.

Kit was going to the stars.

CHAPTER ONE

Houston, Texas
January 1962

Anne-Marie Smith took in the crates strewn across the floor of her new dining room. She nudged the biggest one with her toe and the contents jingled. Well, she'd never liked the Crown Derby. If the past year and a half had taught her anything, it was that there was no use in crying over spilt milk, broken china, or shattered marriages.

She looked up at the movers, four large men who lifted everything as easily as dollhouse furniture—and dropped it just as easily too.

"Can you put those"—she gestured at the crates— "over there, please? I'll deal with them later. And move the table into the middle of the room?"

Doug had picked the china and the table, a huge mahogany thing with a dozen ornate chairs for entertaining all his legal partners and their wives. It was dark and Victorian and didn't fit the new house— though of course neither did Doug.

When the movers had finished, she said, "Let's talk about the sitting room."

Here at least were things she'd chosen: a sleek couch and several chairs covered in a subtle floral pattern. They were crammed in front of the picture window that looked out over the woodsy front yard.

"Lake Glade is *the* neighborhood, darling. All the astronauts live there," her mother had cooed as she'd explained the gift she'd bought Anne-Marie.

"It's a house, Mom! A house I haven't seen!" she'd snapped in response.

It was also a way out of Dallas. So she'd done what anyone would have: She'd taken it and moved her kids to Houston.

"I want the couch there," she told the movers. "And those chairs and the drop-leaf table by the fireplace."

"What about the television?"

There it was, though she specifically remembered giving different instructions. "I'm sorry, but it's not going in this room. I want it in the den."

One of them made a face. "Is that what your husband wants?"

She crossed her arms over her chest, purposefully shielding her left hand. "Yes." She said it as if it weren't a lie. Thank goodness Judge Harper had finally, agonizingly settled the question. All she felt about the divorce—all she wanted to feel anyway—was relief.

But no one would let her, because genus *Divorcee* was too strange.

They'd known what to do with her when she'd been Doug's wife and, before she'd married, Larry McCann's daughter. She'd even been recognizable as a woman who'd kicked her unfaithful husband out. *Whose husband hasn't strayed?* she'd been told more than once. But when you became the woman who hadn't gotten over it, the sympathy turned into hard stares and leers, gossip and silence.

She squared her shoulders and smiled in what she hoped was a fair approximation of her mother's style, all flies and honey and strong Southern womanhood.

The foreman was tall and burly. Looking up at him, she felt her inches' deficit, and the fact she hadn't set her curly red hair in days and needed a shower and was even—horror of horrors—wearing trousers. But this was her house. These were her things. They should go where she wanted them.

After a pause, the movers made some ambiguous noises but did what they'd been told.

A half hour later one of them asked, "What room is your husband going to use as an office? Or do you want us to do the kitchen next?"

Yes, because the kitchen was her office. Anne-Marie clenched her hands into fists and shoved them into her pockets. "You know? I'll finish. With my husband." So she'd be on her own for the unpacking, then, but that suited her fine. "You've been so... helpful."

Ten minutes and some paperwork later, the movers drove away and she walked through the house again. Her house. All right, a house that her parents had bought, that was filled with her husband's furniture. Details.

She fingered the boxes spread over the counter in the kitchen. After she unpacked, she was going to put up wallpaper. She was going to make all the catalog recipes she wanted, including for weeknight suppers when no one was coming over, just because it would be fun. And—she leaned into the back room—she was going to paint. It was so dark and masculine now. She wanted it to look like her home. Hers and the kids'.

But first, she had to get all the ingredients for their home out of the boxes.

She started in the kids' rooms. She wanted to make things as normal for them as she could. When this was over—when they'd adjusted to the new house and school, when she'd gotten used to working, when she was able to go through a day without the dread of unresolved legal haggling hanging over her—Anne-Marie would never take normal for granted again. She was going to wrap herself up in normal like a rain slicker to protect her from the world.

It took some shifting, but at last she found the box labeled *linens*. Enough tape to plug a leak in the Hoover Dam helpfully slathered it. She pulled on a corner, managing to get a tab free, but when she leaned back, the little piece ripped clean off.

Why had she sent the movers away? They hadn't been too bad... Okay, yes, they had been, but she should have made them open more things first. She didn't have a knife—silly, practical men and their tools—but she did have a nail file. Maybe it would do?

Anne Marie levered the blade into the corner of the box and began sawing through the tape. One inch. Two. Jeez, she'd made an error not starting with a box with knives in it because this was going to take forever.

As she progressed, the box began to rock. She slapped her left hand onto the top to steady it.

"Hold still, almost done," she ordered it between grunts. But before she could get too excited, the nail file shot forward. It sliced through the last few inches of tape and lodged itself into her hand.

For a long second, she blinked at the gash shining garnet on her finger. Then she pulled the blade out and wrapped her finger in her blouse to staunch the bleeding.

"Damn," she whispered, permitting herself a rare obscenity. She blew the hair that had fallen into her eyes off her face. She truly was a wreck.

She stumbled back to the kitchen and nudged her pocketbook open with her elbow. She didn't have so much as a tissue. What kind of a mother didn't have an adhesive bandage or two?

She didn't want to answer that. She also didn't want to meet her neighbors bleeding and disheveled. She'd intended to make something for them, to wear a dress, anything that might negate her marital status. *See: I'm not threatening! I brought a quiche.*

Divorce might be a problem beyond quiche. But so was the cut on her finger.

She took her hand out of her shirt. Blood immediately welled and began to drip. She wrapped her finger up again and, muttering all the way, she pushed the front door open and went in search of help.

Lake Glade wasn't a neighborhood yet—it was mostly open lots. Her and her neighbor's houses sat at the end of a cul-de-sac called Harbor View. They did not in fact have a harbor view; there wasn't a harbor at all, only a big pond. The developer was an awfully good salesman.

A bright white Thunderbird sat in the neighbor's driveway. At least someone was there. She knocked as best she could with her elbow. After several long beats, she knocked again. Inside the house, something thumped and then someone cursed.

A male someone.

Before she could figure out what a man might be doing home on a Monday morning, the door opened and a chest confronted her. A muscular, hair-dusted chest. She swallowed and blinked at the flat, pink nipple inches from her nose.

Anne-Marie tried to process it, the pink nipple and the tawny skin and the golden hair, but before she could, she looked up into the face that went with the chest. The same face stared out from the cover of the *Life Magazine* currently sitting on the coffee table in her mother's house across town.

"Commander Christopher Campbell?" Her voice came out high and breathless.

She'd learned a lot about herself in the past eighteen months: she couldn't abide unfaithfulness; the comforts of her marriage didn't make the rest of it worth it; she could take care of her children on her own; and in fact, she liked being alone.

Most of these facts had been good. But that she got flustered and star-struck when confronted with a shirtless, albeit famous, man? Not welcome.

She focused on his eyes, which were big and blue. Then she dug around for the last bit of her poise. Finding it, she did not allow herself to react as he smiled. Slowly. As if he knew all the things she'd just thought about. Which was, thank goodness, quite impossible.

He spoke. "Usually the women who show up on my doorstep call me Kit."

Oh, that helped. She was less flustered already. Nothing snapped her back to reality faster than the arrogance of a highly sexed man.

From the way he'd said the line, she suspected there were a lot more of them. He may have—he did have—an impressive physique, but that was why she didn't believe in that sort of thing. Doug may not have been so… earthy, but he was plenty good-looking. And that had gotten her nowhere.

If she ever did settle down again, it would be with an absolutely regular-looking man, and preferably not one who answered the door only partially dressed in order to flirt with strange women.

At least Commander Campbell—that was, *Kit*—could probably give her a bandage and a knife. So what if his trousers did cling to his… No, she was not going to think about his hips.

Utterly composed, she said, "I'm your new neighbor. Next door. Anne-Marie Smith."

His smile broadened. "I saw the truck. Welcome."

"I, well…" She looked down. The blood on her blouse resembled a gruesome poppy.

Kit inhaled sharply, evidently noticing her injury for the first time. "Come in."

He slid a hand around her elbow, and with all the skin on display and the blood loss, she felt a bit of a jolt at the contact. *This type of man infuriates you*, she reminded herself.

"We'll get that cleaned up," he was saying, "but my house is, uh, a bit of a mess."

She gasped as she stepped over the threshold. Saying his house was a mess was ridiculous—a horde of toddlers may as well have rioted there.

A chair had been overturned and pillows streamed across the floor. A lamp rested on its side, the shade gone. Food and debris littered the carpeting. Overarching the room was the strong scent of stale alcohol.

Kit gently but firmly led her around the scene of destruction. "The kitchen's through here."

She tried to ignore the crunching every step generated. It sounded as if someone had sprinkled crackers over the floor and then danced on them. Maybe it was some sort of astronaut game.

Luckily, the kitchen was cleaner. Evidently most of the party had been focused elsewhere. Kit propped her against the cabinets and released her. Her arm suddenly felt colder, and she shivered.

"Do you get squeamish at the sight of blood?" he asked as he produced a first aid kit from a drawer and popped it open.

"No." Nearly a decade of motherhood had cured her of that—but she omitted the detail. For some completely silly reason, she was uncomfortable with the idea of him thinking of her as a mother, but of course he'd know soon enough.

"What'd you cut yourself on?" he asked.

"Nail file."

He grimaced appreciatively and poured rubbing alcohol onto a cotton ball.

"This is going to hurt."

She was tempted to say something saucy, but more than she wanted to snap at him, she wanted him to wrap her wound so she could unpack. Sniping at him would have to wait.

With a deep breath, she pulled her hand from her shirt and set it in his. His palm was warm and surprisingly soft. He immediately pressed the cotton ball down on the cut and her eyes watered. She bit the inside of her lip to avoid crying out.

"Shh," he whispered, rubbing her wrist with slightly callused fingers. "It'll be better in a second."

She nodded and closed her eyes. He kept running his fingers over her. She could feel it in her toes— which must have been her body's way of distracting her from the stinging.

His fingertips caught on the bones of her wrist, grazed over the side of her hand, and then back again.

She inhaled, hoping sense might enter her lungs with the air. He was a man: a pretty, vain playboy of a man. This wasn't the time to become attracted.

He lifted the cotton and then reapplied it, pressing harder. "You really cut yourself."

"Yup." She sure had.

The silence stretched out between them. He kept up the rubbing, and her heartbeat fell into rhythm with it.

"You been in the neighborhood long?" She needed to blot out the sensation.

"Few months."

His voice was low, and she felt something pool in her stomach. A frisson of... interest. No! She didn't want to name it; that would make it real.

"Do you like Lake Glade?" It was much safer to talk about real estate.

"It's quiet. I..." He trailed off and then said, "You should know I don't typically hold rowdy parties. I don't want you to think I'll be waking you and your family up."

The last bit sounded like a statement, but she suspected it was a question. Not a prurient one, but curious. He wanted to know about her. He was, after all, patching her up, and they were going to be living next to each other—it was natural he'd want to know.

She wasn't sure how to answer, however. She'd lied about her family to the movers—but she was never going to see them again. She couldn't lie to Kit. He'd find out. Also, he was an astronaut. It would be like lying to G.I. Joe.

"My kids," she said. It wasn't precisely what he'd been asking, but it was true, and it clarified that she wasn't unattached. She wasn't married, but she also wasn't precisely alone.

He nodded. "I definitely don't want to wake up your kids. Also, I'm not a fan of disasters. I try to avoid them, as a rule."

"You don't enjoy scrubbing dip out of carpeting?"

"Not on Mondays."

"But the rest of the week?"

"Wednesday gets boring sometimes."

In spite of herself, she smiled. An astronaut was flirting with her. He thought she was married and that this was only politeness, but still. Most women in America would give anything to be in her spot—messy hair, sliced finger, and all. So for a moment, she let herself play along.

She shook her head sadly. "I'm surprised *Life* omitted that bit."

"Ah, well, you shouldn't believe everything you read." He popped his jaw in what sounded like genuine frustration, but it evaporated when he said gently, "I'll be a good neighbor."

He removed the cotton, and before the blood could start gushing again he had a bandage around her finger. He pulled it taut and adhered it better than she could have done. He wet another cotton ball and used it to clean her up. His movements were lighting quick. Practiced. Confident.

Pilots likely got banged up a lot. He'd probably done this many times, and all the touching and comforting was clinical and unconscious. She'd been the one imagining anything else.

"Thank you," she said as she watched him work. "Nothing's unpacked yet. I don't know what I would have done without you."

"Probably bled to death." He shot her a lazy grin.

She pulled her hand back and glared at him.

"Do you need a clean shirt?" he asked.

The word *shirt* called attention to his lack of one. She didn't permit herself to look at him for more than an instant. She shook her head and trained her eyes past him at his refrigerator—a turquoise Frigidaire that gleamed in the corner and made her covetous. Hers was plenty nice, but that was a beauty.

Still not looking at him, she said, "I'll pass on the shirt, but I'll take a knife."

He produced a folded blade from his pocket. He wasn't even dressed and he had a knife on him?

"Do you want some scissors too? I'm sure I can find some."

"If it's not too much trouble."

He pulled open what appeared to be a junk drawer and fished around inside. He finally located a pair of sewing scissors identical to the ones that were in her mending case in a box somewhere inside her house. He held them out to her, but when she reached for them, she stumbled toward him. Her cheeks heated.

Maybe she wasn't imagining the flirting—but that was all the more reason to get out of his house.

"Can I get you anything else?" he asked.

"No, you've been very welcoming," she said through clenched teeth. "Or you will be once you give me those."

"I'll have to have your family over for dinner once I, you know, have the carpets cleaned." He handed the pocketknife and scissors over with a broad, polished smile. He clearly felt as if they'd reached a détente.

All she said was, "Hmm."

As she followed him out, there was another noise to accompany the crunching of crackers: a door opening. Into the midst of the carnage in Kit's living room strode a woman wearing a frothy peignoir and nothing else.

The woman was young, blonde, and extremely pretty. Her hair was tangled and her makeup blurred—not particularly surprising, given what had evidently gone on here—but she bounced in all the right places.

If the *Life* article was to be believed, Kit was unmarried. And indeed he wasn't wearing a ring. The woman, presumably not his wife, was unmoved by it. All of it. The mess. Anne-Marie's presence. The blood all over her shirt. Kit's evident absence from his bed.

The young woman just scratched her head and smiled at them. "Morning."

Anne-Marie glanced at Kit, who had flushed scarlet. When he didn't say anything, Anne-Marie offered, "Right. Good morning. I was just going. Thanks for the, uh, bandage. And the knife. And the scissors. I'll bring them back when I'm done."

She wrenched the door open before he could respond and strode back across the yard. She'd been hoping for a new start in Lake Glade, but she should have known that men were the same everywhere.

Without feeling even a hint of disappointment, she started opening boxes and putting together her home.

Kit Campbell found himself wishing for a large broom. One big enough to sweep all of this mess away with a flick of the wrist.

A rustling rose from his sofa, chiffon against leather. Miss Delancy, taking a seat as she too surveyed the damage.

The broom would have to be big enough to entangle the problem of Miss Delancy in its bristles along with the rest of it. But there was only Kit and his two hands.

He spotted a heavy tan trench coat lying across the chair, much too much coat for a Texas winter. She ought to try some of the blizzards from his youth in Nebraska—now *they* had been cold.

"You didn't bring anything else to wear?" he asked.

"No." The word floated up from the couch. "They told me to come in my nightie and the trench."

They being Carruthers and Storch, two of his co-astronauts. Miss Delancy was their idea of a present.

Well, last night he couldn't refuse. This morning, with her flitting among the wreckage of the house, the bloom was off. Which was why, even though he was unmarried, he preferred his trysts to happen in hotels—he could up and leave when it was done. No awkward morning-afters.

He lifted the trench coat from the chair, causing a landslide of beer bottles. The crash of them stabbed into the ache between his brows. A green one came to rest against his bare foot, stale beer dripping onto his big toe. Henkins had brought those, some kind of European beer. But the fancy label didn't make it taste any different from Budweiser to him.

He nudged the bottle away and carried the coat over to Miss Delancy. Her bouffant had transformed into a nest that could have housed several families of rats, and her eyeliner was now mostly underneath her eyes. The smearing of her mask from last night revealed she was younger than he might have guessed.

"Why don't you put this on? I'll find you something to wear and we'll call a cab."

She stood and slipped the trench around her thin shoulders, keeping her gaze on the floor. She settled back into the black leather couch and gave the living room a sad glance before offering him a wistful smile. "Kind of a mess, huh?"

"Yeah." He wasn't certain if she meant the state of the house or if she was including herself. He stepped back, something hard snapping under his bare foot and digging sharply into his heel. He bit back some foul words. It was in fact a damned mess. "I'll just go rustle up some clothes and call a cab."

"You know," she said, a hopeful spark entering her gaze, "I'm free tonight. Or this weekend. If you wanted to get together again."

Aw, hell. Another point in favor of hotels—he could get clear before this kind of talk started up. See a woman a second time and she might start thinking she was going to be on the cover of *Life* too, right next to her astronaut husband.

"We'll be real busy with training this week," he said. They would be, not that his training schedule ever slowed his nighttime activities. "I'll call you if I get a moment." He gave her a charming smile to ease the sting. "I'll just go get those clothes."

He picked his way across the living room toward the hall, dodging stale crumbs, empty bottles, and crumpled party hats. He straightened a picture, a modern thing with different-colored blocks. The one in the lower corner flamed orange. Mrs. Smith's hair was that same color. And her freckles—she had a veritable Milky Way of freckles scattered across her nose and cheeks.

Yet another lady he'd disappointed today. He'd seen her expression when he'd made that joke about calling him Kit. But she'd called him Christopher—which he hated—and she'd mentioned *Life*. His facade was thinning these days.

Perhaps he ought to go help them unpack when he was finished with this mess and introduce himself to Mr. Smith. Funny that Mr. Smith didn't have a pocketknife handy. And hadn't helped her bandage that wound. Kit frowned.

Given the looks Mrs. Smith had been giving him, or rather his chest, Kit didn't think Mr. Smith was keeping her too happy. Kit had never slept with a married woman before—there were so many single ones to choose from—but the way Mrs. Smith had looked at him made him reconsider.

He scrubbed a hand through his regulation crew cut as he walked into his bedroom. No, better not sleep with Mrs. Smith. The awkward mornings after would never end if he bedded the woman next door.

Not to mention her kids. A sour taste filled his mouth. He never really knew what to do with kids. If all of America expected him to be a hero, the kids expected him to be a god. He wasn't, which made interactions with them awkward. And now he had a couple of them living next door.

He rummaged in his drawers for something suitable for Miss Delancy, coming across two more copies of that stupid magazine lying on the dresser. He tossed them onto the growing pile at the back of his closet, cover after cover of himself along with the other five members of the Perseid Six—the astronauts, the ones who were going to help America win the space race.

For some reason, people wouldn't stop bringing him the magazines, thinking they were doing him some kind of favor.

He settled on some sweatpants and one of his undershirts for the girl. Not quite respectable, but better than her current getup.

He took the back way through the hall to the kitchen, not wanting to face Miss Delancy again just yet. He pulled the phone book from the cabinet next to the phone, flipping to the C's. As he did, his gaze landed on the spec manual he was supposed to be reading today, the edges curled and sticky with... beer? He lifted it to his nose and sniffed. Beer. Parsons was going to love that.

He set the spec manual aside. It would have to wait until the house was back in order. And after he'd helped the Smiths.

Which didn't leave much time. He tapped a forefinger against the cover consideringly. Parsons was already on his case; Kit didn't need to give the man any more reasons to bust him down from backup on this mission. Because if anything happened to Joe Reynolds—not that he wanted anything to—Kit was going to space.

He took his bottom lip and rolled it between his teeth at the thought. Floating in zero G, the stars ever present, Earth beneath him—he'd be breaching a frontier few men would ever see.

His breathing went slow and deep, his eyelids coming to half-mast. He'd do it someday—not as backup, but as mission lead. All those years learning to fly, the nightmare of Korea, the rigors of astronaut training, hell, even Parsons and his foul temper—it would all be worth it, once he was floating in the stars.

But first he needed to call a cab and clean up this house. Earth life was so damn mundane.

Once the cab company was called and Miss Delancy had something more suitable to wear, he let the dog out of the bedroom where he'd been contained. Then Kit took the trash bin in one hand and began clearing away the debris. As he was tossing away a plate of chicken wings that had taken on a stomach-curling smell, Buckshot came trotting up with a scrap of something blue and filmy in his jaws.

Kit dropped the trashcan. "Bucky, sit."

The pointer's butt hit the shag carpet, but he held on to his prize.

"Drop it."

Bucky hunched his head in protest, but eventually released it. Kit held up the scrap, pinched between his thumb and forefinger. A shirt? A lady's shirt?

He tossed it into the garbage. Whomever the owner was, she wouldn't want it after it'd been in Bucky's mouth.

"I don't even want to know where you got that."

Bucky trotted off, liver-spotted haunches wiggling with supreme unconcern.

"And don't you dare eat any of those chicken bones!" Kit shouted after him.

"What?" Miss Delancy called from the bathroom.

"The dog," Kit explained.

"What?" she called again, even louder.

Kit shook his head and wished the cab would hurry up and appear. Sometimes a man just wanted to talk to his dog in peace. "Nothing," he yelled back.

He tossed more trash into the bin, including what might have been more women's clothes and three more copies of *Life*, and set aside keys that someone had left. Bucky, for his part, licked industriously at some dip smeared into a rug.

Kit cleared the sideboard in the dining room with one sweep of his arm, delighting in the juvenile joy of it. His mother had insisted he needed the massive thing, along with the dining room table, the china, and the living room set. Sleek and modern, "space-age furniture for a space-age man," the salesman had said.

He preferred his ancient sofa in the den. After spending his Navy career in assigned housing, it was still odd to have a house all his own. The developers had offered the houses practically free to the Perseid Six, and he would have been crazy to turn one down.

Miss Delancy came out of the bathroom after a time, wearing his clothes—or more accurately, swimming in them—her makeup washed off and her hair somewhat tamed. And looking even younger than before.

"Can't you just leave this for the housekeeper?" she asked before yawning widely.

"I don't have a housekeeper." He replaced a lampshade, poked a finger through the hole torn in it. He twisted it toward the wall. Good as new.

Her eyes went wide. "But you're not married. How do you take care of this? Or cook?"

Another illusion shattered. Heroes didn't cook. Or clean. Or use the toilet.

"I manage," he said lightly.

A honk sounded from the front drive. The cab. Thank God.

"Your ride is here," he said, trying not to sound as pleased as he was.

Bucky went to the door to bark furiously.

"Yeah, I already know," Kit said as he opened the door for Miss Delancy. Wrapped in the trench, his sweatpants pooling around her ankles, she looked like a modern urchin. They filed past his T-Bird in the driveway, Bucky running off to investigate the bush by the mailbox. Kit winced at the scuffs marring the car's paint. He hoped they'd buff out—yet another chore to put on the list.

The cab was waiting at the end of the driveway, rumbling like a monstrous bumblebee. The driver, an older gentleman, helped her into the back with old-fashioned courtesy. But when he turned, he pursed his lips and gave Kit a disapproving shake of his head.

Kit held his tongue. Instead, he waved to Miss Delancy as the car pulled away, keeping his smile pasted to his face. Only once the car was out of sight did he let himself sag.

Now just to finish the house. And then be a good neighbor.

He turned to look at the Smiths' house. Through the windows he could see her watching him, his pocketknife held in her hand, her finger wrapped in gauze. She looked pissed. At him?

As he watched, her fist tightened on the handle of the knife, something more coming into her expression. *Awareness.*

Huh. She was definitely attracted to him. And she was angry about it. Or maybe she was angry at Miss Delancy. Or Mr. Smith.

Interesting. He liked redheads, particularly those who looked at him with so much fire.

He put on the "most charming smile in America," bland though it was, and punctuated it with a wave. She was his married neighbor—best to tread carefully.

He saw her nostrils flare in a sniff even from here, before she turned away to attack another box.

Well. Looked like he wasn't going over there, at least not if he didn't want to be disemboweled. It was

for the best; he'd wait until Mr. Smith showed himself. There was no need to get caught alone with Mrs.
Smith again, or caught up in a messy affair—no matter
how intriguing he found her.

He turned to go deal with his ever-increasing chore
list, the image of her hand clenched tight around his
pocketknife, the bandage stark against her skin, stuck
in his brain.

CHAPTER TWO

Nobody ever expected space exploration to generate all this paperwork.

Kit sighed and shuffled the reams and reams of it on his desk in the office he shared with the rest of the Perseid Six, trying to bring a bit of order to the chaos. Or at least reduce some of it.

People thought the life of an astronaut was one of nonstop excitement, one thrilling mission after another, interspersed with sessions of rigorous training. No one ever imagined an astronaut spending his time reading dusty technical reports. Or sitting at a typewriter and pecking out a test flight report with two fingers, as Carruthers was doing right now.

Pluck, pluck, pluck. Astronauts were proficient in everything except typing.

Ding. He'd hit the end of a line.

Swish. The carriage return.

Those noises were more likely to be part of Kit's day than the roaring whoosh of several tons of rocket fuel igniting, propelling a man past the atmosphere into the void beyond.

"Did you like your present?"

Kit turned to find Carruthers smirking. He was slim, with blackish-brown hair that had a habit of curling at the ends. He always wore it just a little too long—not enough to get called out, but long enough to let everyone know what he thought of regulation haircuts. *Life* had said he was "screen-idol handsome," and the ladies who kept him company each night likely agreed. The choice of Miss Delancy made sense: she was Carruthers's type.

"She scared me half to death when she jumped out of the closet." Kit said it lightly, as if it were a prelude to a funny story—one he didn't intend to finish. Kit wasn't one to kiss and tell. Besides, Carruthers had a different woman in bed each night. He didn't need the birds and the bees explained.

"Aww, were you so scared you'd disappoint her?" That was Storch, putting in his two cents' worth. "Maybe I ought to give her a call."

Kit let his snort answer that. Everything Carruthers did, Storch had to do one better—an arms race of sex. Storch was the joker, always acting as if everything happened solely for his amusement.

Dunsford, a few desks down, put in, "Maybe she'd like my number."

"You're married," Kit pointed out mildly.

"Why'd you have to remind me?" Dunsford whined. "And thank you for breaking up the party at one and sending me home to the ball and chain."

"Obviously a fate worse than death." Kit tried to keep his tone sarcasm-free. Dunsford had chosen to get married; he couldn't complain he hadn't the freedom the single guys did, not when he'd brought it on himself.

"Precisely," Dunsford said.

Kit picked up the spec manual, the pages brittle and warped and still smelling of alcohol. He'd read it yesterday, but it wouldn't hurt to look it over as many more times as he could before the test tomorrow. Parsons would be hunting for even the smallest infraction after how the last test had gone. Engineers were so touchy about their equipment, even if they couldn't drive the stuff.

"Though Margie did say she met the woman who bought the house next to you in the neighborhood," Dunsford said.

Kit turned around. He was the only one with a new neighbor. "Oh? Both of them, or just the missus?"

Dunsford snorted. "There is no Mr. Smith. Mrs. Smith"—he placed mocking emphasis on the *Mrs.*—"is a divorcee." He said it extravagantly. *De-vorce-ay.* Each syllable came out as lascivious, as if the word itself was a scandal.

Huh. So there was no Mr. Smith. Which explained why Kit hadn't seen him.

Which meant... He tapped the spec manual on his knee. There was nothing in the way of their attraction. Nothing at all.

Except for the fact she was his neighbor. And she had kids. He tried to avoid women like those.

"Can you even imagine what she must be like?" Carruthers said. "A woman who'd actually leave a man? Or who was so shrewish that he left her?"

Kit frowned. Mrs. Smith hadn't exactly been nice—her final glare at him from the window had been positively livid—but *shrewish*? "She seemed okay."

Every head turned to stare at Kit.

"What's she look like?" Storch asked, his smile tipping into a leer.

"She's..." He searched for a description, but all that came to mind was that carrot hair and all those freckles. Freckles on top of freckles, scattered across her nose and cheeks.

But the other men didn't want to hear about freckles. They wanted something more risqué. "She's attractive. On the shorter side"—he remembered how he'd had to bend down to bandage her finger—"but if you like redheads, she'd be your type. Kind of like Debbie Reynolds."

There. That should sound disinterested enough. He didn't want to dissect Mrs. Smith with the guys, not in the way they wanted to.

"Who's also divorced," Storch said.

"Hey," Dunsford protested. "That wasn't her fault."

"A redhead!" Carruthers snapped his fingers. "I knew it. Told you she was a shrew. What did Margie say?"

Kit suppressed his grimace and tapped the manual faster against his leg.

Dunsford shrugged. "That she was standoffish. I don't remember much else. You know Margie, I can't keep track of all the words that come out of her mouth."

Standoffish. Yeah, Kit could see that. But Mrs. Smith was alone in the world, without a man—she'd had to come to Kit when she'd cut herself. He ought to go over tonight and see if she needed any help. A man's help.

"You'll have to keep us informed," Carruthers said, in a way that made it clear he'd make a move on Mrs. Smith if conditions were favorable.

Oh hell no. If Kit couldn't make a pass at her, Carruthers certainly couldn't. "She's got kids."

Every man in the room deflated. Kids looked at them like they were heroes. Like Superman, the Lone Ranger, and Buck Rogers all rolled into one. It was hard to pursue a lady when her kids had a shrine devoted to you in their bedroom.

"That's that, I guess," Carruthers said.

Kit tried not to be pleased at the defeat in the other man's voice. It wasn't like he could make a play for Mrs. Smith either, but Carruthers went through women like tissue. He'd run over Mrs. Smith.

Carruthers took up his typing again, the noise seeming to hit Kit right behind the eyes with each keystroke.

"Jesus," Storch muttered. "I've already got a headache."

"You young fellas can't hold your liquor," Dunsford said. At the age of thirty-six, Dunsford was the oldest of the Perseid Six—and he could drink a prodigious amount.

"A headache?" Carruthers asked, still pecking at the typewriter. "Isn't that what your girl from last night said too?"

Storch gave him the bird.

Kit picked up the spec manual and flipped back to the description of the heat shield.

Silence fell as all four men went back to their paperwork. So much paperwork.

His mind slipped into the rhythms of the spec manual, the jargon becoming a fluent language as he immersed himself in it, until—

"Campbell."

It wasn't loud, but then Parsons didn't need to shout to make him jump.

As darkly sallow as ever, the lead Perseid engineer stood in the doorway. With his white short-sleeve button-up and thick horn-rimmed glasses, he was the most engineer-looking engineer Kit had ever seen. Given his job, it was only fitting that the man looked as he did, but he didn't have to be so smug about it.

Parsons also hated Kit—all the astronauts actually—which made their encounters just that much more pleasant.

He sneered at the spec manual in Kit's hands before marching over and snatching it up.

"What did you do to this?" His nose twisted as his sniffed. "Is that liquor?"

Kit snatched it back. "It's mine, so what does it matter?"

"It matters because you're sloppy. It matters because this is yet another symptom of how you approach your test flights. It matters because carelessness like this will cause missions to fail and people to die."

All of the noise in the room had ceased. Every Perseid astronaut had frozen and was fixed on Kit and Parsons.

Kit ground his teeth. "You can't engineer something like this to be failsafe. There's going to be failures and errors—it's never been done before. And as to the danger, you're strapping a person onto a rocket and sending him into a vacuum. Of course it's dangerous. We all accepted that."

"Parsons, I know you don't understand," Carruthers said, "but we're all military men here. And pilots. Don't wrap us in fucking swaddling."

Storch added, "We're not monkeys. When things go wrong, *we* actually know what to do. Thanks to all the training you force on us."

"If you think some beer on a spec manual is the end of the world for this mission..." Dunsford shook his head.

Parsons's nostrils flared. Kit just kept staring him down, knowing that all the other men had his back. Nothing united the Perseid Six faster than their dislike of Parsons.

"Look," the engineer said, "this isn't flying toy jets trying to set some kind of silly speed record."

"Hey!" Storch held one of those speed records, and he wasn't pleased to hear it dismissed.

Parsons ignored him. "The entire world is watching. We fail, and the Soviets win. And you may not care if someone dies on these missions, but I certainly do."

With that, Parsons turned on his heel and left. Kit's fists shook with fury. How like that bastard, to give a speech like that and just run off. He was always trying to ensure he got in the last word. Kit threw the spec manual onto his desk, sending one of the hills of paperwork crashing down.

Yes, as a test pilot he'd done some dangerous things. Been in a few bad crashes. They all had.

But he wasn't reckless. And he wasn't sloppy. No one knew his aircrafts like he did. It was why he'd been chosen for this mission.

He didn't just hop into a jet prototype and push it to maximum acceleration. He'd been an aviator of skill and art and study—still was. Parsons could stuff it.

If he weren't relying on the man to recommend him for lead in the next mission, Kit would have told him that.

The clack of the typewriter started up again. Kit hadn't even been aware it had stopped.

"Ignore him," Carruthers said, never looking up. "He's probably not getting laid on the regular. Binds him up like that, and then he takes it out on us."

Kit snorted. "Why don't you put a girl in *his* closet, then?"

"No girl deserves that," Storch said with a laugh.

Kit silently agreed as he buried his face back in the spec manual. No matter how he felt about Parsons, he did have to read this manual. Beer or no.

And he'd have to check on Mrs. Smith at some point. Ask about her finger.

Just to be neighborly.

Anne-Marie closed the back door and leaned against it. For two days she'd opened boxes, more boxes than she remembered packing. They'd multiplied on the way here, probably somewhere around Waco. Weird things were always happening in Waco.

She'd made beds, put together bathrooms, and filled cabinets, but the house still didn't feel right. She kept waiting for the alchemical thing to happen. The home-making thing.

When she'd married Doug, she'd moved into his place the day after their honeymoon. She'd put down rugs, hung pictures, and set books on his previously bare shelves. But the space had remained foreign for weeks.

Then one day she'd been out shopping and had thought, *I can't wait to go home.* Doug's house was her home.

She'd thought she could make that happen instantly here, but it hadn't.

Even the kids felt it. They'd tried to be happy, but anxiety laced their words.

"Look, Mom, room for all your pans!" Freddie had said, gesturing at the cabinets as if shelves were a major technological breakthrough.

"And the backyard is huge!" Lisa had added.

Think of the children, everyone had said. Almost all Anne-Marie did was think of the children. The children were why she'd thrown Doug out and why she'd refused to take him back.

The children are fine, she'd insisted—all while suspecting they weren't.

Seeing them trying so hard to please her, she knew that they'd understood the depth of her unhappiness, no matter how hard she'd tried to hide it. She owed it to them to be happy, not merely to act like she was.

Maybe it would be better when they started school? Except then she'd be starting work. Her at work—ha! The thought was strange and freeing and itchy all at once. When her dad's friend Mr. Chambers had offered her a place in his travel agency, it had seemed silly to refuse. What else was she going to do? And while there was money from Doug and her parents, she wanted to be independent.

She'd even let the kids eat dinner while watching television tonight. She'd hoped it would feel daring—everyone with a tray, in front of Red Skelton. Who needed that too-heavy formal dining room?

Instead, it had felt like they were each eating on their own. Like they weren't a family.

She set a cigarette between her lips and fumbled with her lighter. She flicked it three times but no flame emerged.

"Need some help?"

She looked toward the shout. Across the darkness, sitting on his back patio, she could make out the outline of Kit Campbell. He'd been watching her for who knew how long. Of course.

She sighed and walked over to him. "Um, sure. If you don't have company."

"I'm alone." The intimacy of the words pricked her skin.

He stood and fished a lighter out of his pocket. She stepped closer, trying not to think about the lack of space between them. The lighter crackled to life and she leaned into its glow. When her cigarette was lit, she looked up at him and inhaled sharply. His eyes were intent on her, searching for... something.

Before she could decide how to respond, the lighter snapped shut and they were plunged into darkness. She exhaled and could hear him shuffle away and then sit.

"There're some more chairs if you want to stay."

She didn't. But she also didn't want to go back to her house, back to the laundry and the quiet. So she fumbled until she found a chair as far from his as she could get.

"How's your finger?" he asked.

She flexed it. "Better, thank you. I'm done with your pocketknife and scissors. I'll bring them back soon."

He didn't answer, and so she looked up into sky. The moon was bright, floating in a great spill of stars. More almost than she remembered seeing. In her old Dallas neighborhood, there was too much light to make much out up there. She glanced across the patio at Kit Campbell, astronaut, but he was little more than a silhouette in the darkness.

"Do you often sit in the gloom?" she asked after a bit.

"There's a light"—she could hear him gesture—"but I didn't want to bother anyone."

She laughed. "You didn't have any neighbors until two days ago. Who would there be to bother? Or is it that you like the night sky?"

His chair creaked uncomfortably. Oh. She'd figured it out.

Without drawing attention to his non-answer, she craned back. There were so many stars. "What's up there tonight?"

"Let's see... I'd guess you know Orion. But over there, to the right of it, is Taurus. The bull."

All she could see were a million points of light. They were pretty, sure, but she didn't know what made any one special. "Over where? What am I looking for?"

"Follow Orion's belt. It points to a—well, to something that resembles a letter Y centered around a bright red star. The points are his horns and his face."

She squinted and puffed on her cigarette. Without much conviction, she said, "I see it."

She understood why people were interested in space, but it had always felt like a test she failed. She looked up and saw... well, beauty. Vastness. But she didn't see a bull. *The emperor has no clothes.* But you couldn't say that to an astronaut.

So for a long time, they sat in silence. She puffed and watched the sky until she could, really could, see Orion taking aim at something. She stared at the flashing star, which did have a red tint. And she listened to the man across the patio breathing. Listened to him until she felt like she knew his mechanics.

But before she could figure him out, a furry form padded over to her and flopped its head into her lap.

"You have a dog?" She didn't mean to sound so horrified, but it, the dog—were dogs so big?—was slobbering in her lap.

"May I introduce Buckshot?" She could tell Kit was trying not to laugh.

For herself, she was still trying to get used to the idea of a thing drooling in her lap. With all the dignity she could muster, she said, "I'm very pleased to meet you."

Kit did laugh then. It was a warm, ingratiating sound that pooled in her stomach. The sensation increased when, in a husky voice, he said, "He can smell your fear."

She considered sticking her tongue out at him. Kit, that was. The dog wouldn't care. She could have gotten away with it under the cover of darkness, but grown-up ladies were supposed to behave better. She just reached up and gingerly rubbed Buckshot's ears.

The dog rolled his head to the side and made an appreciative noise, which only deepened as she rubbed harder.

"Well, at least you're very soft," she told Buckshot. He rubbed his head against her lap and grunted. Since he wasn't running away, she assumed that was affirmative.

When she looked up, she could tell Kit was watching her. She looked down, back at the dog, and ignored Kit's gaze, heavy now on her.

"See, you're a natural." His words creaked. Not with disuse, though that too, but with… something else.

Without looking up or acknowledging it, she responded quickly and lightly. "I am not. The kids want a dog, and I keep telling them no."

He scoffed. "Why? Kids and dogs go together like peanut butter and jelly."

"Says the man who doesn't clean his own floors."

"I do too."

"Hmm." Her tone suggested that she didn't believe him—which of course she didn't. Doug certainly had never cleaned a floor. Neither had her father.

She shook off the things she was feeling and turned the conversation back to the stars. They were safer. "What's that bull called again?"

"Taurus."

A few more seconds of silence passed, then lightly she asked, "Is that where you're going, Commander Campbell? Up to the stars?"

"It's Kit. And yeah, that's where I *want* to go."

He didn't sound proud. The words weren't a brag—though he would have earned it. No, they were a bone-deep wish.

"Do you enjoy being an astronaut?"

"Yes," he said after a long pause. And then he didn't elaborate.

She'd learned the art of conversation in her mother's River Oak sitting room. The key when talking to a man was always to ask about his job. *What do you do?* followed by *Oh, that sounds hard.* Those two comments could get a woman through almost any dinner party. They opened a door, and then they flattered.

But Kit evidently didn't know the rules.

Well, if he didn't, then she didn't need to follow them. "You'll forgive my observation, but that's fewer words than *Life* generated about your smile."

Her mother would be howling over that, but Anne-Marie didn't care. She'd seen the man half-dressed, seen the woman he'd partied with. She could tease him.

"They sure can type over at *Life*." His tone was mild, but she felt the embarrassment and the frustration underneath it. He didn't seem to like the magazine's commentary about him, and he liked even less her bringing it up.

"It is charming, you know. Your smile. Your entire affect, really," she said soothingly. "And if it gets you to the stars, well, who cares what they write?"

"I didn't say it wasn't worth it."

She wasn't sure how to respond. Most of what he'd said to her felt polished, like lines he used often, but this was different, not at all like in the *Life* interview or like a line he'd drop on a woman. He was still, almost rigid, as if he hadn't meant to say the words and was surprised by himself. And if that were true, she wasn't sure why he was sharing them now.

She was even less sure of what to do with them. When he knew so little about her—she wasn't even certain if he knew she was divorced—the conversation felt lopsided. She could feel his vulnerability. She didn't like it.

"You don't think they'll beat us up there?" she asked.

"The Soviets?" A different kind of vulnerable, that question.

He shifted in his chair. She could feel the weight as he considered that. The heavy pause as he didn't answer.

Oh God. Maybe the Soviets were further ahead than anyone realized. Maybe they would conquer space. The kids—what would happen to them, to all of them, if that happened?

"Of course they won't," he said. Jaunty, confident, but not nearly enough to fill the silence he'd created after her question. "How could we not win with the astronauts we have?"

She set her jaw. That wasn't a real answer—she'd heard that exact same line in every press piece about the Perseid Six. Whatever honesty he'd been giving her had vanished, though perhaps this was a requirement of his job.

Then he said, "Do you need any help? With the move?"

The balance between them shifted again.

She sat up straighter. "Someone told you?"

"That there's no Mr. Smith?"

She crossed her legs and then her arms, and Buckshot stumbled away. "There is a Mr. Smith. He just isn't *my* Mr. Smith."

"Yes," Kit said very softly. "Someone told me."

"I don't need any help."

"All right."

She snuffed her cigarette out on the paving stones and rose. "I don't know why everyone has trouble believing that I'm fine on my own."

She started to storm off, but he stood and caught her hand in both of his. He was warm, much warmer than anyone should be on a February evening, even in Texas.

"I mean it." The words abraded the skin of her wrist, and the fingers of her free hand curled. "I'm willing to help you. With anything."

The bastard. It wasn't that she hadn't had this offer before. Oh no, the main thing men seemed to know for certain about divorcees was that they had unfulfilled... needs. And they were just the men for the job.

The only thing that was different this time was that some tiny voice inside her wanted her to say yes.

Thank goodness she was too old to listen to it. "I wouldn't want to trouble you." Her voice dripped with condescension.

He ignored it. "No trouble at all." He dipped his head as if he were going to kiss her arm.

She snapped her hand back. "But can you fit me in? Let's see, you have the stars, all of Houston's blondes, and that's not to mention *Life*. You're a busy man, Commander Campbell."

And with that, she flitted home.

CHAPTER THREE

The next morning, Anne-Marie knelt in the nearly empty flowerbed in front of her house. She was taking a break from the unpacking to plant daffodil bulbs. That was what she needed: bright explosions of yellow. Her mother was convinced that it was too late in the season and they wouldn't bloom, but Anne-Marie was hopeful.

She must be over the divorce. Sad, lonely divorcees didn't go in for bulbs—the payoff was too far away, and flowers brought romance to mind. She was happy enough to handle the wait and well-adjusted enough to think of love without bitterness. By the time these daffodils bloomed, this would be a real home for the kids and her. She knew it.

She finished digging a spray of holes, then grabbed a small bag of sand and went about tipping a bit into each. When that was done, she clambered to her feet to find the bag of bulbs. Her movements were a bit slower than she would have liked. Her thirties were creeping up on her. She could shake her head to dismiss the thought all she liked—time marched on. But never mind her thirties! She was putting in bulbs. Or she would be once she found them.

She shook her leg, trying to wake it up, and her knee popped as if to spite her and emphasize that she was going to age no matter what.

"You're not that old," she said to her knee and herself.

But when she turned—where had the bag from the hardware store gotten to?—she found Kit Campbell, he of the space exploration and the fruitless propositions, standing on the sidewalk watching her. He was dressed as if he were planning to go for a jog. Of course he jogged. That was how he maintained his playboy body.

Her jaw clenched and she clutched her trowel more tightly. What did he want?

"I wouldn't say you're old at all, Mrs. Smith," he called. He licked his lips and let his eyes travel down her body. When he made eye contact again, he lifted a brow in admiration.

It was too much. He was just trying to annoy her now. "How comforting, Commander Campbell, coming from a man of at least forty."

"Thirty-four."

She knew his age well enough thanks to *Life*, but she enjoyed making him correct her.

He didn't seem annoyed, however. He was mostly trying not to laugh—and this infuriated her even more.

"What are you doing?" he asked.

"Planting bulbs."

"Need any help?"

Her answer was a stern "No."

He put his hands up in surrender. "Have a good morning then."

It will be once you leave. She didn't answer him. She merely smiled as coldly as she could. And when he left, she went back to planting hope—which had nothing to do with the astronaut next door.

Nor did it when she was struggling to get a floor lamp out of her car the next day. Her car was parked in her driveway. She needed to remove the lamp and put it into the house and get over to her mom's to pick up the kids or else bedtime was going to be entirely too late.

The lamp had other plans.

The man at the furniture store had helped her load it, but now she wasn't sure how he'd made it fit. She craned into the car and tapped around beneath the front seat for the cord. If it was tangled on something, that might explain her difficulty.

And sure enough, when she found it, the cord was wrapped around some sort of support beam under the seat. She gripped it as best she could and tugged. Her hand, slick with perspiration, slipped off. She tried again. And again. But it was to no avail. The lamp wasn't moving.

She wedged herself further in the back seat. She was outright kneeling in the car, though it was quite possible that neither she nor the lamp were ever going to get out.

She tugged and tugged on the cord and then grunted in frustration.

"I keep finding you in such interesting positions."

The fact was, she could get out. When she knew Kit Campbell was staring at her bottom, she could be quite speedy indeed in extricating herself from her car.

"Do astronauts ever work?" she demanded as she attempted to straighten her curls.

"No." He shook his head apologetically. "We drive around town bothering people and *not* preparing to go to space."

Actually, he was dressed as if he were going out: crisp white shirt, charcoal gray suit, skinny ultramarine tie. He could be headed out to accompany Anita Ekberg to dinner in that getup. Ekberg seemed like his type.

Anne-Marie tried not to think of how she always seemed to be at her messiest around him.

"Are you so desperate to get your scissors back that you keep finding excuses to bother me?"

"That's it. I'm useless without them. The future of the American Space Department is in jeopardy."

He crossed his arms over his chest and smiled at her. It wasn't precisely the *Life* smile. It was too rakish for that. America might not like this version of Kit— though a certain segment of American women would probably think it was just fine.

"I'll go get them and you can cross me off your list in the future. All the way off." It wasn't like she could sit around in the dark trading confidences with a man like Kit.

The mirth in his face evaporated. "I was only joking."

His words seemed… earnest.

For a few seconds, she considered apologizing, but then she remembered: He'd insulted her far worse when he'd propositioned her. And he'd never apologized for that.

Instead she sighed. "It's been a long week." This was true. She only had one more day before starting her new job, and the house wasn't nearly finished.

He nodded. His eyes were still full of concern, his brow slightly furrowed. She couldn't decide if this was better than his naughty innuendo or not. "Moving always takes longer than you think it will," he said.

"We'll be settled soon."

"Where are your kids?" He glanced around.

"My mom's."

"Your parents are in Houston?"

"Yes, River Oaks."

"Oh." He was clearly not a Texan and so didn't know what this meant. It was a relief he wouldn't imply that her father's money made her life possible, even if it was true. "Do you—" He gestured toward the car in an obvious offer of assistance.

"*No.*" She hadn't meant to sound so emphatic, but she no longer felt bad about being firm with him. He, like everyone, thought she was incapable.

He watched her as a chef might a new recipe simmering in a pan: closely, trying to make her out, with a bit of appraisal. He didn't seem repulsed, and certainly she'd given him reason to be. He seemed intrigued— and not entirely lustfully.

Astronauts were odd.

He gave her a half-salute. "Duty calls, then."

He climbed into his Thunderbird and drove off, leaving her with a stuck lamp and some confusion.

The confusion was still present when she got to her mother's. Freddie, precocious and still so much a little boy at nine years-old, was sitting on the couch reading the Perseid Six issue of *Life* for approximately the forty-seventh time.

Kit Campbell was following her.

"Did you have a good day?" she asked as she kissed him.

He made a face. "Pretty good. Grandma had us help her polish silver." He looked into the dining room and wrinkled his nose.

"Ah." She'd gotten roped into that game a time or ten in her childhood. "Always makes you feel accomplished, though."

Freddie looked at her as if she'd said something wild.

"Mom, look at this," Lisa called.

When Anne-Marie went into the dining room, her seven year-old daughter held up a hand mirror. It was the kind that paired with a brush and comb, all three meant to be displayed on a dressing table.

"It's pretty," Anne-Marie said.

"Part of my mother's trousseau," Anne-Marie's mother put in. She took the mirror from Lisa and smiled at it lovingly. She turned it over in her hands and brushed her fingertips over the rosebuds engraved on the back.

Those were the kinds of flowers Anne-Marie still felt bitter about. The entire thing, actually: the performance and stage props of proper womanhood.

Anne-Marie released a scoff as loudly as she dared. Sometimes, especially since the divorce, it felt like she and her mother were from different centuries. Kit might one day leave the planet; her mother still saw a woman's life as the accumulation of silver-backed mirrors. Neither world had much to offer Anne-Marie.

She turned from her mother to her children. "We need to get going." Over her shoulder, she said, "Thank you for taking them, for feeding them."

"My pleasure! When I found that house, I wasn't thinking of how far away it was. I really should have pressed for something closer."

Thank goodness you didn't. "I like the house." Well, she would when it was unpacked. And when she figured out how to handle Kit...

"Have you met the neighbors?"

"Not yet." And she hadn't met the neighbors; she'd just met the one. "Not all of them," she amended. As much as she might not understand her mother, she loved her and she hated lying to her.

"Well, I've heard it's a very friendly place."

Lake Glade hadn't existed long enough to develop a character, so Anne-Marie suspected this was a real estate agent's tale. As a group, they'd never met a house or a neighborhood they didn't like. Reality didn't matter.

"Are you ready for school tomorrow?" she asked as she drove the kids home.

"Yes." Lisa packed an awful lot of introspection into the one syllable. She was ready, but she was also nervous.

"I'm sure both of your teachers will be nice. And you'll meet lots of kids, and pretty soon you'll have friends here."

In the rearview mirror, Anne-Marie watched Freddie fingering the interior of the door. He didn't say anything. He didn't even offer token agreement.

It had been right to leave Doug. It had been right to leave Dallas. But some days, it was hard to remember that.

"You'll see," she promised.

Kids moved all the time, even kids whose parents didn't get divorced. But she could do better than that. "How do you feel about some ice cream?"

Freddie popped up and smiled, big and true. "Really, Mom? We already had cookies at Grandma's." Freddie was ever honest. He hadn't yet learned to lie.

"Just this once."

But an hour later, Anne-Marie was willing to consider instituting an "ice cream for dinner every night" rule if it could make such a difference. Freddie was animated in a way he hadn't been in weeks as he spooned whipped cream onto his sundae. Lisa belly laughed so hard when they were playing pinochle on the living room floor afterward that they had to take a break.

Dairy products were all it took? Evidently.

She lingered in the bathroom while they got ready, watching them brush their teeth and squabble over counter space. Then she tucked them in—an hour later than normal—and kissed them.

"That was fun," Lisa sighed, already mostly asleep.

"The most fun we've had in a while," Anne-Marie agreed.

But no answer came back to her.

She cleaned up the living room and the kitchen without once glancing toward the back door—or in the direction of the astronaut next door.

CHAPTER FOUR

Like spilled gin, the allure of work evaporated quickly for Anne-Marie. Mr. Chambers's travel agency was large, disorganized, and colorful. Around the room, a number of men and women talked excitedly into phones. Stacks of brochures threatened to explode from every surface. Posters lined the walls touting exotic vacations. *Try Nice! See the Grand Canyon! Sunny Spain!*

Anne-Marie was certain that if she stayed here for any length of time, the chaos would induce insanity. Or perhaps the woman Mr. Chambers was talking to would bury Anne-Marie beneath all the papers, where she wouldn't be found until someone needed prices for luaus in Waikiki. The woman's expression said she might consider it.

"Oh, Mrs. Smith, I didn't know you were starting today." The blonde held herself rigid as a column, her military posture at odds with the full pink skirt and perfectly matched heels. But her glare made the voluminous crinoline appear less festive.

Anne-Marie tried to smile, but the blonde's expression just tightened. So Anne-Marie swallowed and fumbled with the buttons on her coat. The other men and women in the office were watching the exchange curiously. It was a test, then.

Anne-Marie examined the blonde, taking in more than the woman's clothing and displeased mien. She wasn't wearing a ring. It was hard to say whether the ones with the rings were more bitter than the ones without—which didn't make much sense. Divorce couldn't possibly threaten this woman if she weren't married.

Mr. Chambers, apparently unaffected by the woman's tone, beamed at them both. "Roberta! Just the person I wanted to see. I'm certain I mentioned to you last week that Anne-Marie would be here today. You'll show her everything, right? Get her all settled in?"

"Uh-huh."

That was ominous.

"Great!" Mr. Chambers responded. "We'll go to lunch about noon, okay?"

Anne-Marie blinked a few times. Oh. He wasn't speaking to Roberta. "Of course. That would be lovely. Thank you."

She didn't want to have lunch with Mr. Chambers. She wanted to learn what they meant for her to do here and then to master it. And if she could, she wanted to get home early so she could cook a decent meal for the kids. They'd need it after their first stressful day at school. But even she knew that keeping the boss happy was important, so she'd have lunch with him.

With a little wave, he jogged off, leaving her alone. Well, as alone as one could be with Roberta.

The other woman twitched her skirts and turned. There probably should have been rustling, but there wasn't. Eerie. She started off, and it took Anne-Marie a few seconds to move after her.

"You'll be back here," Roberta explained when they reached a desk in the back corner.

It had a typewriter, a phone, several large bound books, and a mound of papers: impersonal and intimidating at once. Roberta gestured, and Anne-Marie sat. She immediately regretted it. Now she was at a height disadvantage, but then she generally was.

Several seconds passed before Roberta said, "I wasn't expecting you until tomorrow."

Maybe the other woman's frustration didn't have anything to do with Anne-Marie's marital status or the nepotism that had led to the job.

Trying to use the opening to change the tone, Anne-Marie said as apologetically as possible, "I'm sorry about that. I can come back."

"No, you're here now." Sadly, there had been no change. "What we're going to start you with is the airline reservations. This is the backlog. Honestly"—she leaned close, as if imparting a secret—"most of the girls can't make heads or tails of them."

Anne-Marie wasn't certain how she felt about being a girl, but she did know that she'd rather be in the group than out of it.

"Um, okay." She began flipping through the papers.

Roberta set a hand on top of the stack to stop her. Maybe the order was important. "Those are the schedule and rate books. Any flight that anyone can take anywhere in the world is in there. And these"—she tapped the papers—"are the flights we need to book."

"My word." It was a quite a stack.

Roberta then explained how, once you knew the flight you wanted for the client, you called the airline to schedule the flight and then entered the information into the sheet before returning it to the appropriate agent for filing. The tickets followed in the mail a few weeks later.

"Start with this one," Roberta said, picking up the first paper from the stack. "Locate the flights in the schedules, write them down on some scratch paper, and then find me. If everything is right, I'll show you how to call."

"Seems easy enough."

Almost immediately, Anne-Marie wanted to revise her pronouncement. Nothing about this was easy. There were about five hundred ways to get from Houston to Istanbul, and none of them made any sense with the other items in the couple's itinerary. Maybe they could drive up to Dallas instead. Anne-Marie could put together some notes on the best restaurants.

She glanced around. There must be ten people working for Mr. Chambers. Whatever Roberta might have said, Anne-Marie was confident they could all do this. So she could do it too.

At the bottom of the stack of books, she found a volume with explanatory notes and tables. Once she'd figure out how the columns were organized and the airport codes, she finally located the correct pages for the departures and then for the arrivals.

Within a few minutes, she had a series of flights that seemed to work. Newly humble, she crossed to Roberta. "Is this all right?"

Roberta inspected the notes and then looked up. "It'll do." She didn't even try to keep the shock out of her voice.

Anne-Marie wanted to crow, but she swallowed the impulse. It wouldn't help. Not really. All she said was, "Oh. Good."

"Let's call TWA."

Once the call was half over, they were put on hold. "You should start with the next one while you're waiting," Roberta instructed.

Anne-Marie took the next page from the stack and shuffled through the rate books, trying to find the right one. "How long does each reservation take?"

"Once you get the hang of it"—Anne-Marie doubted that would ever be the case—"about forty-five minutes."

Anne-Marie hadn't taken much math since high school. The two years' worth of home economics classes she'd taken at UT before leaving to marry Doug hadn't included anything but the numbers used in cooking. But despite her deficiencies, forty-five times all those papers... was a big number.

For the rest of the morning, Roberta checked her work, for which Anne-Marie was grateful. The other woman might not want her there, but Anne-Marie would rather not make a mistake.

The morning passed quickly. After a nice, albeit quick, lunch with Mr. Chambers—who insisted on calling her Annie and suggested that things with Doug might still blow over—she tackled more of the stack.

She wasn't sure how many weeks of reservations it represented, but she might not ever catch up, particularly not when people kept bringing more of them over to her.

Maybe it was a hazing. Maybe when she finished the last one, they'd induct her into the team.

Mr. Chambers came to usher everyone out just before five—so much for the idea of getting home early—and Roberta said begrudgingly, "Good job. You're getting the hang of it."

"I'm grateful. You've been so helpful." Only one of those things was true.

She trudged out to her car. She'd never wanted a job. At school, she'd met women who did seem to envy their boyfriends. Bookish women who liked to talk about anthropology and who burned their cakes. Anne-Marie had been in awe of them even as she'd known she wasn't one of them.

It made the current situation a tad funny. She was working. Outside the home. For money. And once she got the people at work to see that she wanted to be good at it, she wouldn't even be sorry. It was one more important step toward independence. And for that, she'd put up with Roberta's attitude.

When she pulled into the drive, her appreciation and gratitude burned up. For there in the front yard stood her mother, her children, her next-door neighbor, and his dog.

"Hey, Mom," Anne-Marie said as she climbed out of her car. Gosh, she sounded even more weary than she felt.

"Honey! You neglected to tell me who your neighbor *is*."

Anne-Marie had left that out purposefully. She'd hoped to omit it forever. Maybe he'd just take the partying and the blondes and the big blue eyes and the stargazing and the propositions somewhere else. Maybe she'd never have to tell them about his day job—

"Did you know he's an astronaut?" Freddie demanded, all earnest shock and admiration. "Did you know that he held the highest altitude record in 1957? That he flew thirty-nine combat missions in Korea?"

Did he also mention that he's a cad? But all the frustration she felt evaporated when confronted with her son's brown eyes. "Fancy that." She pulled the boy in for a hug. Over his head, she said, "Good evening, Commander Campbell."

"We've been over this, and I'm starting to get a touch offended. It's Kit."

His voice scratched in the right places and rubbed in the rest. As if he hadn't been annoyingly kind and then made a pass. As if he hadn't been a bother as she'd unpacked for a week.

"He's going to go into space," Lisa said, helpfully breaking into the moment.

"I didn't say that." Kit shook his head. "I'm the back-up for the guy who's going to go into space."

And how he must hate that. She smiled at the thought.

Freddie broke the hug and turned around. "But the next one, the next mission, that's when you'll go right? Tell me about the rocket. Is it true what I read about the modifications to the control panel?"

She glared at the back of her son's head. "Where were you reading about the control panel?"

"In *Boy's Life*. But is it true?"

"Well, you know, I didn't read that article," Kit said. Unease held his smile tight, a pause stretching as if he were searching for the next thing to say. "How about you tell me about it?"

Freddie launched into a breathless summary, with Lisa assisting with revisions now and again. Clearly she'd read the piece too. Anne-Marie watched the recitation skeptically. Kit nodded along, his smile sticking, although he didn't look quite easy. At least not as easy as he had when he was teasing her the other day.

"How was work?" her mother asked eventually, proving that even when it came to impressing the astronaut next door, there were limits to how much technical talk she could abide.

"Oh, fine."

"Where do you work?" Kit asked.

She looked up, feeling her cheeks heat. Something about him knowing, and wanting to know more, made feel self-conscious. "Uh, Lakeview Travel."

"You're a travel agent?"

"Well, I am now."

She needed a little more practice talking about work. His question was a perfectly reasonable one, and somehow it brought out the worst in her. Which fit: pretty much everything about him brought out the worst in her. Though that bit might be mutual—she hoped he at least felt guilty realizing he'd hit on a woman with children.

"She's decided to go to work since… you know," her mother tacked on. The divorce was still incomprehensible to her mother. In the eighteen months since Anne-Marie had thrown Doug out, she hadn't heard her mother use the d-word more than three times.

Anne-Marie rubbed her brow, half to soothe the headache that was beginning to boil there and half to hide her face from Kit. "Yes. Well. Let's say goodnight to the astronaut, kids. You can talk to him about the control panel later on."

"But we haven't thrown the ball for Bucky!" Lisa whined.

She looked down at the dog, who'd wandered over and lolled at her feet halfway through the control panel discussion.

At the sound of his name, Bucky lifted his head. His tongue sprawled out and trailed on the ground.

And the children wanted one.

"Um, tomorrow maybe."

"It'll have to be later this week, kids," Kit said. Was that relief? "Tomorrow I'm off for the Cape."

"That's in Florida," her mother said.

"I know that." Anne-Marie was a travel agent, after all. She had a handle on geography. "I hope you have a good trip." At least this meant she'd be spared him, and his voice and late-night conversation and his come-ons, for a few days. Maybe when he returned, she'd have figured out how to keep him in the detached, neighborly box in which he belonged.

"What about Bucky?" Freddie asked.

"My friend Carruthers is going to watch him."

Oh good. For once Kit was helping her out.

"The astronaut Carruthers?" Lisa asked.

Freddie said, "He's a great pilot."

"Does he live near here, too?" her mother asked. "This neighborhood truly is splendid."

It was as if her family had never met men who wanted to strap themselves to big rockets and fly out of the atmosphere before.

Kit took all of this in stride. It probably happened to him all the time. "Yeah. He's over on Harbor Wind."

"Does he need any help with Bucky, do you think?" Freddie said. "'Cause we could walk him."

"I'm sure he'd like that."

No. One astronaut was enough. More than enough. "Commander. That is, Kit?"

Despite the noise and the questions and all the people vying for his attention, when she said his name, he
snapped up and looked right at her. "Ma'am?"

She wet her lips with her tongue, needing a moment
to work up to it even though she'd already decided to
ask. "If Carruthers could be persuaded... I, that is we,
would be honored to watch Bucky."

"Oh, Mom! Really? Can we?"

"Yes!"

"Anne-Marie, are you sure?"

Again with their Greek chorus bit. Anne-Marie
raked a hand through her hair, messing it up, but who
cared? She was losing her grip on reality—a few flat
curls were the least of her problems.

"If Commander Campbell says it's okay," she ground
out.

"I'd appreciate that." He offered it with a smile she
could feel as much as see. A smile she didn't want to
return, but she knew that she did.

The taste of it was stale, however. Kit might be—
was, in fact—good at it. The charm. The convivial,
public persona. But Doug had been, too. On a lesser
scale, of course. In a minor key. But she'd seen that
film, and once was enough. The kids might like him,
and they might covet his dog, but she was keeping this
friendly and remote. She was just going to watch his
dog. She didn't want to encourage his... inappropriate

propositions, even if—especially if—they made her body tingle.

"All right then. I'm going to go make something to eat. Freddie, if it's a good time, why don't you head over to the Commander's house and see what..." She looked down. Bucky was snoring loudly against her shoe. "... what the dog needs for a few days. Take some notes. And be home in twenty minutes."

"Yes, Mom. I will. Absolutely. An astronaut's house!"

Imagine that.

CHAPTER FIVE

The capsule hit the water with a mighty splash, the great hand of inertia shoving Kit hard into his restraints before throwing him back into the chair. He took a few deep breaths, waiting for his brain to stop jiggling as the capsule bobbed in the waves.

"Reentry complete," he said for the benefit of those listening on the radio.

It wasn't really a reentry—Kit and the capsule hadn't been orbiting the earth. Rather, the capsule had been dropped from a helicopter so he could drill on egress procedures.

Drilling, drilling, and more drilling. He hadn't drilled this much even as a midshipman at Annapolis.

He disengaged the tubing attached to him, then freed his head from the helmet, finally stripping off the awkward gloves.

"Give me a few minutes to finish up my notes," he said to the waiting helicopter pilot. The notes weren't absolutely necessary; it was all part of trying to make it as real as possible. But Parsons never met a bit of data he wanted to leave behind, so Kit took readings, wrote his own impressions of the landing, and went through the dreaded checklist. God, he wished he had his Juicy Fruit. But no gum chewing was allowed.

He made one last notation, opened his mouth to tell the chopper pilot he was ready—

A loud thud rattled the capsule, followed by the *glug* and *whoosh* of water pouring into something.

Fuck me.

The hatch had blown. Much too early. He was supposed to blow the hatch manually, but only after the helicopter had secured the cable to the capsule. But whatever explosives Parson and his crew had put on the bolts had blown without him triggering it.

And that rushing gurgling? The waters of the Atlantic Ocean filling the capsule.

In the half second before his training kicked in, his mind brought forth the image of Anne-Marie's hand clenched tight around the pocketknife, her injured finger starkly white. The snap in her voice as she'd said, *But can you fit me in?*

Now what the hell made him think of that?

Then his mind became nothing but one sustained instinct—release this, disconnect that, grab that other. All the while, tickling at the very back of his skull, was the continuing rush of the sea, pouring into the capsule, pushing it down under the waves by inches.

With a scramble and a push, he was out.

The helicopter hovered above him, the blades chopping out a chest-drumming rhythm. He swam from the capsule, wanting to get away from the rotor wash and not be pulled down with the capsule in case it sunk. The chopper stayed with the capsule, the crew trying to snare it for recovery.

The helicopter crew's first priority was the capsule—the astronaut was expected to fend for himself, thanks to his buoyant suit.

Except his suit wasn't keeping him up. Water was pooling in the wide collar, and he was sinking—a little slower than the capsule was, but just as surely.

He began to swim, kicking and pulling with all his might, the drag of his suit making the effort an order of magnitude harder than it should have been. But if he stopped, he would die.

The waves slapped at him, shoved frigid water down his throat, pushed him under the surface, making him splutter and gasp each time his face hit fresh air. He forced his arms and legs to keep moving, to keep crawling toward survival.

Another chopper appeared on the horizon. Rescue.

The second helicopter hovered above him, a crew member leaning from the open bay to lower a cable. Kit caught it, clutching with all his strength. As he was pulled toward safety, he slowly became less pure survival instinct and more himself again. He looked toward the capsule as he went up.

The chopper had hooked on the capsule, but wasn't pulling it up. Instead, with each roll of the ocean, the capsule slipped further beneath the surface. The ocean pulled at the capsule like an angler reeling in a fish, only in reverse.

For several long moments this tug-of-war continued, the chopper lifting the capsule back to the surface in a moment of calm while the ocean pulled it back with the slap of a wave.

As Kit reached the second chopper, it became clear that the first chopper was losing the struggle. The ocean was going to take the capsule and the chopper along with it—unless they released the cable.

The crew member pulled him into the bay, seawater sluicing from his suit to splash across the floor. Kit sprawled for a moment, sucking in air as the chopper roared around him. His chest ached from swallowed saline and his ears throbbed from the decibel level, but he had to know what was happening. He shoved himself to his feet, his suit making him as ungainly as a walrus on land, but he managed to grab a strap to steady himself as he turned back to watch.

The first chopper was even lower now, the capsule completely submerged. The cable released then, snapping in on itself like an angry snake, and the first chopper began to gain altitude.

Beneath the water, Kit could see only a glimmer of white before the waves rose again, drowning the capsule in a smear of green-gray and pulling several million dollars' worth of equipment to the ocean floor.

Parsons was going to be pissed.

Parsons was more than pissed—he was damn near having a stroke.

Kit had dreaded this moment the entire flight from Florida to Houston. It was turning out to be even worse than he'd expected.

The entire engineering team was assembled. Kit sat on a stool in front of them. Only the dunce cap was missing.

It was meant to be a debriefing, but Kit knew it for what it really was: a disemboweling. Of him. And why not? A very expensive test capsule had been lost on his watch, even if it wasn't his fault.

Parsons paced the front of the room, his face beet red and his neck swelling—actually swelling, like a bullfrog's—with the force of his anger.

"Why the hell did you prematurely blow the hatch?" he asked for the tenth time.

"I didn't," Kit answered for the tenth time.

"That's impossible. The bolts wouldn't have blown on their own." Parsons paced back and forth, turned and paused. His left foot pawed at the ground before he started off again with goring force.

"Of course." Kit couldn't keep all the sarcasm from his tone. "Nothing ever goes wrong with explosives, does it?"

"Explain to me why these things always go wrong with *you*. Are you just unlucky? Or are you sloppy? This little accident lost us an entire training capsule. If we send you into space, will you have another little accident? What will you lose then? An entire rocket? Someone's life?"

Christ. This incident—which wasn't his fault—might cost him his only chance to go to space. He gritted his teeth and tried to think of something, anything, even remotely conciliatory to say, something that didn't admit his guilt. But all that came were more hot words, which he kept behind his teeth.

"Um? Excuse me?" One of the younger engineers was tentatively raising his hand. A big guy, who ought to have looked like a linebacker, but the hunch of his shoulders and the shy cast to the eyes behind his glasses gave lie to that. Kit searched his memory for the man's name—Jefferies.

"What?" barked Parsons.

Jefferies stood, somehow looking small even at his full height. "Well, if he had triggered the hatch himself, wouldn't he have burn marks on his hands? From triggering it? Since you can't do it with the gloves on?"

Kit held his hands up high, so that everyone could see, turning them back and forth. A silence fell across the room as everyone took note of their unblemished state.

Parsons stared at his hands, Kit holding them before him, defiance rising within him. After a moment, in which Parsons's face went from red to black, the head engineer tossed his clipboard to the floor and slammed the door as he marched out of the room.

Later that day, Kit drove home in his T-Bird, which still sported scuff marks. He probably should have been more mollifying in the debriefing. He certainly shouldn't have rubbed Parsons's face in his stainless hands. But hell, he was screwed no matter how this went. Once those explosives detonated, his goose had been cooked.

He turned his car into a hard right, the rear tires squealing as they tried to keep in contact with the road. He pushed the accelerator further down, powering through the skid.

As he reached the gates of Lake Glade, he pulled his foot from the accelerator. Couldn't go tearing through his own neighborhood.

The sight of his garage was unutterably soothing. Three days on the coast and then being called out by Parsons—he was battered, bruised. Or at least his innards felt that way.

He ought to call someone up, like Miss Delancy. He still had her number. Some female companionship would make him feel better.

Or no, not her. He didn't even need to call someone, really—he could simply walk into a nightclub. His fame meant he'd never have to go home alone if he didn't want to.

He slammed the car door. That was what he'd do—get a shower, change, then head right back out. Enjoy some of the benefits of this astronaut business.

Buckshot came bounding around from the backyard, looking over the moon at the sight of him. His own heart lightened at the sight of that familiar brown masked face. The Smith kids had obviously taken good care of him while he had been gone.

The Smith kids themselves came bounding after the dog.

Kit tensed. Their mother was fickle at the best of times, and he wasn't really in the mood for a bout of hero worship from the kids—especially when he wasn't feeling the least bit heroic.

"Hey, Commander Campbell!" Freddie yelled.

"How was your trip?" Lisa asked.

"Fine." He definitely couldn't go into specifics about the failed training run. *Please don't ask any more questions.* But of course they would. That was what kids did.

"Look what we taught Bucky to do!" Lisa snapped her fingers at the dog, who came to attention. The girl pulled a treat from her pocket and slowly placed it on Bucky's nose.

Bucky froze, the treat balancing on his nose.

The dog remained still as stone until Freddie said, "Okay." Then Bucky tossed his head and caught the treat between his jaws.

"How the h—how did you teach him to do that?" Kit wouldn't have said that Bucky was ill behaved, but he'd never dreamed the dog could do something so controlled and fancy.

"We'll show you." Lisa grinned, and Kit found himself grinning back. Maybe spending a little bit of time with these kids wouldn't be so bad. At the very least, they could teach Bucky a few things.

They played with the dog for at least half an hour, trying to teach Bucky to roll over, Freddie demonstrating for the dog as Lisa twirled her wrist and said, "Roll over! Roll over!"

Bucky just barked and ran in circles around them, while Kit watched in amusement.

Perhaps the key to figuring out how to handle kids was to get a dog involved. Too bad he couldn't take Bucky with him everywhere he went.

"Kids! Dinner!"

At their mother's summons, the kids waved goodbye and dashed off to their own house, leaving Kit and Bucky alone in the deepening dark of evening.

The idea of going out had lost all of its appeal, so he ate a Kraft Dinner at his table alone, the silence of his house nearly as heavy as the ocean waves had been.

He washed his few dishes as the sun set, not bothering to turn on the lights as darkness stole throughout the house. He changed from his suit and slacks into an undershirt and some running shorts. They were perhaps too cold for a winter's evening, but after the suffocating press of his astronaut suit, the weight of it as it tried to drag him under the waves—

He wanted as little on his skin as possible, even if he might freeze.

He slipped out the back door, Bucky following along behind.

Sipping his beer, the bottle hard against his lips and teeth, the alcohol cold as it slipped down his throat, he studied the stars. Bucky settled at his feet, a warm mass anchoring him as he stared up at that distant expanse.

A door clicked open—the Smiths' back door. Light spilled out, then Mrs. Smith herself followed, her arms wrapped around her as defense against the cold.

He held as still as he could. But Bucky barked anyway.

"Oh." She said it so flatly and unwelcomingly, he might have been a skunk she'd stumbled across.

Okay, she was still pissed about that pass he'd made at her. Which was silly, because as far as passes went, it had been half-hearted. She should save her anger for something he'd meant more.

Maybe it was the crack he'd made about her age or the way he'd leered at her ass. But in his defense, it was a lovely ass.

"Hello." He kept his tone light. Just two neighbors meeting by chance.

"Hello." Not an inch of give there. "I was just... looking for something. But I don't see it out here. Goodnight."

A clear lie—she hadn't known he was out here, and she was avoiding him.

"Wait." She might be angry, but he didn't want to be alone. And she was better company than none. If he could convince her to stay.

She stopped. "Yes?"

"I'm sorry about what happened. I didn't..." He choked on the rest, realizing how terrible it would sound.

"Didn't mean it?" The disbelief in her voice was sharp. "So you just unthinkingly proposition every woman you meet?"

He didn't want to ponder her explanation too deeply. Or why he'd unthinkingly propositioned her when he'd been resolved not to. "Like I said, I'm sorry. And it won't happen again."

"And the teasing?"

"I'm sorry for that too."

She waited with her hand on the door, her shoulders hunched, her limbs tense. His apology hadn't worked after all.

He dug deep then, went past the charm, the confidence, and into a deeper part of himself, the part that didn't know what to do with her kids or her disdain. And he put that into this next: "I truly am sorry. About all of it. I was an ass. It won't happen again." He spoke that last so slow and distinct, each word could have been its own sentence.

She remained unmoving, her stance unaccepting. His heart slowed.

Then her chin came up. Her shoulders came back. Her hand left the doorknob.

"How was your trip?" A neighborly enough question, but her tone was stiff.

Terrible. He released a deep sigh, his heartbeat accelerating back to where it should be. "All right."

Surprising the hell out of him, she picked her way across the dark ground between them. She'd changed out of work clothes into a housedress—no girdle. Her bare feet peeked out from underneath her hem.

Standing only a few feet from him, she asked, "Everything okay? I guess you can't go into detail."

He remembered his motions as he'd prepared to escape the sinking capsule, all of it done without conscious thought, all of him focused on doing his duty.

Yet, at the very back of his brain, somewhere just above where his neck met his skull, there had been fear. Fear that the ocean would drag him down as surely as it was dragging the capsule, the both of them coming to rest forever on the bottom of the ocean floor.

"Just fine." He flashed his *Life* smile.

She turned away. "Good for you." Her voice was cool. She might have accepted his apology—at least, he thought that was what had happened—but they weren't anywhere near friendly yet.

"Thanks for taking care of Bucky. I appreciate it." Dogs and thank yous—she couldn't be mad about those.

"It was the kids. Thank them."

"1 will," he said, not letting his annoyance into his tone. "But I wanted to thank you too."

She tilted her head toward him, but he couldn't see her expression. For half a moment he was held by the tilt of her head, the considering stance of her. Would she stay? Would she go?

His breath released as she crossed his patio and sank into the chair. The same one she'd occupied the other night. "Are you going to point out more star shapes that look nothing like what they're supposed to?" A little less cold now, but still grudging.

He laughed. "Do you want me to?"

"No. I suppose I just want to look." She raised a finger to the sky. "See the Milky Way? I've never really looked at it properly before. But now that I can see it I feel like I can't look at anything else."

"The stars will do that to you. You see them clearly one day, and then you wonder why you bothered to look at anything else." Bucky set his head on Kit's knee, his warm doggy breath washing across his thigh. "Imagine seeing them up close."

She turned her face to him, and the fire of her hair caught the silver of the moonlight. "Is that what you want to do?"

Yes. "They're a little too far away for me to do that."

"That doesn't mean you don't want to."

"Wanting something you can't have is a waste of time." He should have let go of that impossible, childish dream ages ago. And yet, no matter how often he looked up at those stars and thought how far away they were... he still wanted to see them up close.

And you want to kiss her.

He wouldn't. She didn't like him, and it was clear his offer—stupid and half-assed as it had been—was unwelcome. He knew better than to crash land right next to his own home.

But he wasn't going to pretend he didn't want to seduce her into something other than contempt for him. That he didn't want to hear her whisper his name, heated, needful.

As if she knew what he was thinking, she said, "Hmm. You don't strike me as a man with a lot of unrequited desires. I suppose everything you want falls right in your lap. You being a celebrated hero and all."

"That's right." The bitterness of those words twisted his tongue. "Everything I want just falls into place. I only have to snap my fingers"—she flinched at the sound—"and a genie appears to grant my every wish. All through school, officer training, a damn war, everything just fell into place."

Silence spread between them.

"Sorry," he said after some moments. "I shouldn't have snapped at you."

"I shouldn't have assumed that your life was perfect." There was clear respect in her voice now, which was a step in the right, albeit chaste, direction.

"It isn't perfect at all."

"I know you can't talk about specifics, but can you talk about any of it?"

He pondered that. An aviator wasn't meant to ever admit that anything might be wrong, that he might have doubts or fears. You got in that plane, did your duty, and always counted yourself lucky to do so. You were part of an elite brotherhood. No one dared complain about that.

And the brotherhood of astronauts? Not even a hint of a hairline fracture could appear there. It all had to be smooth as butter. Perfection in every way.

Anything less and he wasn't getting into orbit. It was that simple.

"This test..." He sighed. "It didn't go as planned."

"Ah." She pulled out another cigarette, and without thought he had the lighter out, the flame held up to the tip. As if he'd been lighting her cigarettes for her his entire life.

Had her husband lit her cigarettes like that? A flick of the wrist and fingers, the simplest of motions really, but he felt as if so much more was contained within. At least when he did it for her.

"I suppose with something like this," she went on, "things don't always go according to plan."

He shivered as if he were floating neck-high in the Atlantic. "No, they don't. But you didn't hear that from me."

"Mm." She rearranged in the chair, and he found himself staring at the soles of her feet, illuminated by the light she'd left on at her house. They were dirty, perhaps from the walk over, and he found it endearing as hell. "I'm the Queen of Things Not Going to Plan. I certainly never thought I'd end up, well, here."

He doubted she meant an astronaut's house. He hesitated before asking, "Are you... are you happy that you left him?" Perhaps she wouldn't answer. Perhaps it was too intimate a question based on their short acquaintance.

She took a meditative drag on her cigarette. "Happy? That's tough. I don't know about happy. Would I do it again?" She took another puff, the smoke curling from her nostrils to fade into the black of the sky. "Yes." She ashed the cigarette with a quick, decisive flick. "Now it's my turn. Why do you want to go to the stars so badly? Is it just for the thrill? The glory? To get on the cover of every magazine in the world?"

He knew the line he should give, the one that ASD wanted him to give. *It's all for God and country. It's to win this race to control the heavens in the name of freedom.*

"It's because of a book," he said instead.

"Pardon?" As if it were shocking that he could even read.

His cheeks warmed. "Well, several books, actually. Books about adventuring among the stars." She said nothing. "Like *A Princess of Mars*. Stuff like that."

"You want to go to Mars?"

"Yeah. I want to go see all of it. Suns, moons, planets, comets, novas, nebulae—wouldn't it be amazing to just spend the rest of your life traveling to places no man's ever seen?" He thought it would be. Always had.

She tilted her face back toward the sky, and he knew she was looking at the Milky Way again. Him? Well, he was looking at her neck. "I suppose it would."

"Maybe someday that will be possible. But for now, I'll be happy simply to orbit Earth." A lie. He wanted more. He wanted the impossible.

"Will you get the chance?"

He was only the backup for this mission, and given the mishap on this training run, Parsons would probably like nothing more than to send Kit back to Pax River on the next transport. But he couldn't admit that it was unlikely. Not to her. Not to himself.

He looked up at the Milky Way, the two of them studying the pearly smear of it across the sky. Stars upon stars, all gathered together there, sending their light to this little planet circling an ordinary star.

"Yes," he answered. "I will."

CHAPTER SIX

Anne-Marie sipped her coffee and played with the heavy, flowered drapes. She'd made them for another house, another window. Heck, it felt like another woman had made them. Twenty-one-year-old Anne-Marie wouldn't recognize the thirty-year-old version. Maybe she'd ditch the drapes for shades and complete the transformation.

She tugged them all the way open and considered. Was she a drapes woman? Had she ever been?

Before she could decide, someone else came into the picture. To be precise, he ran across it. Kit Campbell: astronaut, all-American man, and stone-cold fox.

She'd discovered Kit's jogging schedule earlier in the week. She'd noted the time he went out and his route so she could avoid him.

He made, as far as she could tell, two laps. And for the second, he sometimes wasn't wearing a shirt. Or he'd pull it up and use it blot his face. It was... glorious. In a very silly, very coarse way that she was going to get around to chastising herself for one of these days.

And she hadn't positioned herself in front of this window at 6:44 in the hopes of catching him. No. Absolutely not.

Then he did it. He pulled his shirt up to wipe his face, and the muscles of his back rippled like water on the pond down the street. Just golden and splendid. It was even better when he did it running toward his house and she could see his stomach.

She sighed, then slammed her hand over her mouth as if he could hear her. Of course he couldn't, but she flattened herself against the wall just in case. It wouldn't do for him to catch her watching.

In fact, this was it: the last time. If she happened to be looking out the window and he came past... no, definitely not. If he came past, she was going to close the drapes—or the shades—and go into the other room. Because he was just like the rest of them.

Wasn't he?

When they'd met and he'd patched her up, and again during their first conversation under the stars, she'd thought she'd had him pegged: cad, playboy, jerk. During her first week in the house, he'd done nothing to convince her this view of him was wrong.

But after last night, she wasn't sure. She hated not being sure.

She levered herself up and watched his figure retreating down the street. The intentional pump of his shoulders. His hips, slim and insistent. He ran fast, it seemed to her, as if he was excising something from his body.

"What are you running from?" she whispered.

Or maybe he was running toward it—the stars, maybe. Fame. A room filled with blondes.

Whatever it was, it wasn't her and that was fine.

The phone rang then, which saved her from having to think about him anymore.

"Smith residence," she answered.

"Good, I caught you before work."

She set down her coffee and raked her hand through her hair. "Good morning, Doug." She managed to say the words evenly. "How are you?"

"Busy. Which is why I'm calling. I'm not going to get down there this month."

She took a deep breath. And then another. She shouldn't be surprised. Even before she'd left Dallas he'd been finding excuses not to see the children.

"Uh-huh."

"It's this case. It's just... it'll be better in a few weeks."

He believed it and he didn't. He knew it was a lie, but he hoped someday he'd stop telling it. Doug wouldn't ever change.

"I didn't tell them you were coming." She wasn't mad, simply weary.

"Oh, well that's good. They won't be disappointed then."

"That's what you have to say about this? It's good I've lowered their expectations—and mine—so that no one is disappointed?"

"What do you want me to say?"

That had been his big question during the divorce. After a muttered *sorry*—which was an apology that Anne-Marie had found out, not that he'd been involved with his secretary—it had immediately turned into *what do you want me to say.*

The sad part was that she didn't know. The divorce hadn't left her devastated or feeling betrayed. It had made her feel foolish that she'd gambled the most important choice of her life on a man who, in the end, she could let go of without much pain.

No, the hurt and anger had come less from Doug than from everyone else. When woman after woman told her to stay with Doug, that this was, if not okay, then expected—that was when she got angry. When men told her that she would fail without a husband—that was when she was more convinced than ever that she had to leave.

"I don't want you to say anything." She slid down into the chair by the phone, too tired at this point to stay upright. There was no point in scolding him—he wasn't going to change, and it wasn't her problem anymore.

"Are you okay?" he asked. "Do you need anything?"

She knew that the offer was genuine. He didn't seem to have any hard feelings about the divorce, either—which was how she knew it had been the right choice for him as well as for her.

"No, we're..." They weren't fine, but they were going to be. "Everything's getting settled."

"You don't need any money?"

"No!"

Why was every man in her life always offering her the wrong things? Why were they offering her anything at all, and when would they stop?

"Okay, okay," he said with a laugh. "You always were prickly."

She guessed she had been. It was that independent streak of hers that no one would let her flash. Until now, at least.

"Please come see them soon," she said. "They miss you."

He grunted.

She continued. "There's this astronaut next door, and Freddie and Lisa worship him."

Maybe it was wrong to try to make Doug jealous, but she didn't much care. The kids had spent more time with Kit lately than Doug, and that was sad.

"I know what those astronauts are like—all the wild parties and jet-setting. They'll get over it soon."

"I'll have you know—" She stopped herself. She'd have him know what? That Kit wasn't like that? Of course Kit was like that. She'd known it from the second she'd seen the inside of his house, long before the blonde had appeared in the white lace shimmy—who wore something like that? No, there was no reason why she should ever think about defending Kit.

"You're right," she said. "But you should still come. You're their father."

"And I will. When the case is over."

"All right, then. You do that."

"Have a good day." Doug sounded brighter—because he really believed he would. He truly believed that when this case was over he'd change. But he never had before.

"You too."

For a long time after she hung up, she looked at the phone as if it could explain to her the secret of Doug. Of the failure of their marriage, which didn't feel like failure at all. But nothing came to her. It was only a phone and not a crystal ball. And she didn't even believe in crystal balls or fairy tales.

After a bit she looked at the clock and realized she needed to get ready for work and the kids out the door for school.

She shouted to them to make sure they were awake, and when she heard the water running in the bathroom, she drained her coffee.

When she walked by the window, Kit was slouching down the street toward his house, Bucky at his heels. He looked as exhausted as she felt. He wiped his face on his shirt and for a moment she was breathless. He was a beautiful man.

She pulled the drapes closed. Doug might only be right about the one thing—but it was a big thing.

The left rear wheel of Anne-Marie's cart squawked like the release valve on a pressure cooker, at least when it was moving, though it wasn't doing much of that anymore. But when one arrived at the market at three minutes after four—along with everyone else in southeast Houston—one dealt with the only cart available.

She fumbled with her list, a ripped piece of an old calendar covered with notes she couldn't half make out, and attempted to round another corner. But the cart wouldn't budge. She had to pick up the handle and lift the thing, which was ridiculous.

She didn't have too many items left. Maybe she could roll it just on the front wheels the whole time—

"See, I heard he left her."

"Can you blame him?"

Standing in the middle of the aisle were Roberta—who'd spent most of the day subtly criticizing every travel arrangement Anne-Marie had the audacity to propose and the rest asking her to run errands—and Mrs. Cleary, the real estate agent her mother had used to buy the house. Based on the looks they were giving her, she was the subject of their conversation.

She set down the back end of her cart with a heavy click. "Ladies."

"Mrs. Smith," they said in near unison.

For a sticky moment, they all smiled placid, hateful grins at each other. Anne-Marie's was a cork, keeping in the question she wanted to hurl at them: *Why would you take the side of a man you never met?*

But they weren't for Doug, exactly—they were against *her*. A wife was the only thing good girls could be. How many times had her mother said almost exactly that? Anne-Marie had more or less gone to college to learn how to keep house. And then she'd thrown it away.

Any woman who rejected the part—or said it wasn't worth having if it meant putting up with infidelity—became an enemy when she made the rest wonder what they were doing.

Anne-Marie gripped the handle of her cart tighter. These women didn't deserve her anger—though they had it.

She didn't know how to say all that, however: not in any words they would understand.

All she had was, "Isn't it gray out?"

Roberta raised a brow. Mrs. Cleary didn't respond at all.

But she didn't need to, because at that moment, Kit rounded the corner with a six-pack of beer in one hand and a box of cereal in the other. His tie was loosened and the top button on his shirt was undone. The notch in the base of his throat, a perfect little golden indent, winked at her.

He looked haggard and not even a little astronaut-ish. But when they locked eyes, an untroubled smile, a bit indolent but earnest, spread across his mouth.

"Mrs. Smith."

When he said *Mrs. Smith*, she didn't mind so much. Maybe because he looked in her eyes so intently it felt like *her* name, like it had nothing to do with her ex-husband. It wasn't mocking or generic.

It was recognition.

And of course she'd been watching him like a lecher. So when she responded, "Kit," she said it too warm-ly—much, much too warmly. And she probably should have gone with Commander Campbell, because he was a playboy astronaut and the formality would help her remember to keep her distance.

But she hadn't. So Roberta's brow arched up almost into her hairline.

Trying to cover her mistake, Anne-Marie slid into introduction mode. "Uh, this is Roberta Krol, we work in the same office, and Mrs. Cleary, who sold me my house. This is my neighbor, Christopher Campbell."

"Commander." Roberta turned the syllables into a symphony. A seductive prelude.

Something skittered through Anne-Marie's stomach, but she pushed it away. He probably got this twelve times a day, or however many times he interacted with single women. Okay, and probably married ones too. From the moment she'd met him, she knew he took full advantage of all the perks of his job. Roberta's flirtation had nothing to do with her. Nor would it have anything to do with her if he slept with Roberta.

Anne-Marie rubbed at her stomach with one hand.

Mrs. Cleary thankfully had no interest in seducing Kit. She launched into business mode. "You're on Harbor View, right? I think Sally Meyers handled that sale. She always gets all the ASD clients."

"Sally Meyers, yes, that's right," Kit said. He wasn't being rude, but he didn't seem particularly concerned with real estate politics. He turned back to Anne-Marie. "Where are Freddie and Lisa?"

"My mom's got them." She could feel herself flush. It was sweet of him to ask about the kids, but she didn't like these women knowing that he'd asked. It tarnished the gesture somehow.

"I'd forgotten you had children." Roberta clicked her tongue sadly. "How are they holding up?"

"They're fine," Anne-Marie gritted out from behind a rigid smile. "Excellent, actually." She only wished that were true.

"They are indeed." Kit's smile deepened. "Particularly when they're playing with Bucky. I'm sure he'd love for Freddie to throw the ball for him tonight."

He said it so warmly, so genuinely, that she wasn't sure how much he'd heard. Did he understand what Roberta was really asking? What she meant? What she thought? What she was going to think now?

He didn't have to know, did he? He was a man. Doug probably didn't know either, because it didn't concern him. No one thought worse of him because of the divorce. No one thought he was a bad father—and he hadn't seen his children in more than a month.

Which wasn't Kit's fault. But it was time to end this charade.

"We'll see how much homework he has," she said in a voice that made it clear it was too much. "I should—"

But before she could escape, or at least try to with the wheel that didn't work, another woman flew around the corner behind Anne-Marie, boxing her in.

"Kit!" she exclaimed.

Did he know every woman in the area?

"Oh good." The smile he gave the latest arrival was somehow different than the one he shared with her. Friendly. Untroubled. Less lazy. "Margie, I want you to meet my new neighbor. Anne-Marie Smith."

The introduction was, at least from her perspective, unnecessary. Margie Dunsford was famous. She'd been in the *Life* article too, along with the six children she shared with another Perseid Six astronaut. She was pretty, with neat russet curls and a gorgeous tartan dress. The grocery list in her hand was organized into subcategories. She probably never got stuck with the cart that wouldn't work. She probably carried spare wheels in her pocketbook just in case.

Margie Dunsford turned toward her and considered. "We met at the school last week, didn't we? I think your boy's in Billie's class."

Anne-Marie tried to smile. "Yes."

"And you have a daughter too, don't you? She's in Mrs. Green's class, I think."

Anne-Marie swallowed hard and made an affirma-tive noise. She didn't have Lisa's teacher's name down yet.

"Mrs. Green is new this year," Margie said. She wasn't looking at Anne-Marie, but past her at some-thing only Margie could see—probably a chart of all teachers in the area with notes about their efficacy that she kept in her head. "I haven't heard much about her yet. So you'll let me know, won't you?" With that, Margie turned back to Kit. "You haven't sent me an RSVP about tomorrow."

Kit laughed. "Dunsford didn't tell me I needed to. He made it sound more… casual."

Margie rolled her eyes. "I know that you're a bache-lor, Kit, but let me explain to you how it works when you throw a party for twenty-five people that includes a sit-down dinner. I ordered the meat from the butch-er a week ago because I don't like the beef here. Mitch bought the drinks over the weekend. Now I'm finish-ing up with the sides. Do I need to have enough for twenty-four or twenty-five? And men are different than families. I have to calculate different amounts. It affects the cooking, the shopping, the set-up. So if you're invited to a party, you telephone the hostess and tell her if you're going to come." She looked at Anne-Marie and gestured. "Right?"

"Um, yes?" It was right, Margie Dunsford was right—though forty seconds into their acquaintance, Anne-Marie suspected that she was rarely wrong—but something about the other woman's tone put her on edge. Had she passed?

"See? She understands. Wait a second! What are you doing tomorrow?"

It took a minute for Anne-Marie to realize the question was directed at her. "Tomorrow?"

"Tomorrow night? Are you and the kids free? Because the Perrys just canceled, which would leave my kids the only young kids, which they'll hate. But yours are the same age, and you're new and, well, I have extra beef—as we just established. Are you free?"

Anne-Marie looked at Roberta and Mrs. Cleary, who'd watched the entire exchange in petrified silence and fascination.

This was bad. Anne-Marie was already the subject of gossip and speculation. And with Kit... well, it was going to get worse.

But the kids. They'd love to go. She was sure of it. At the very least, there would be astronauts, and Freddie and Lisa couldn't get enough of astronauts. And Margie Dunsford as an ally?

Anne-Marie looked back at Margie. When they'd met at the school, Anne-Marie had been defensive. She'd taken Margie's tone to be prying. But now that she'd seen her in action, she knew that wasn't it at all. If Margie Dunsford had been born a man, she'd be a general. A good one. She was an organizer. And she wanted to manage Anne-Marie.

Well, at the moment, Anne-Marie could use a little managing—at least if it would ease tension around the market.

"We're free. I'm sure the kids would love to come."

"Great! Kit'll give you the details." And with that, the astronaut's wife flew down the aisle, probably to plan parties, dispense advice, and solve US-Soviet relations.

Roberta and Mrs. Cleary exchanged a look.

"Well, I'd better—" Anne-Marie said, but before she could get the entire thing out, Roberta interrupted, "Have a good night, Mrs. Smith."

She and Mrs. Cleary flowed around her stranded cart, doubtless to discuss the entire incident at length next to the cabbages.

Their departure left her and Kit alone.

"So," he said with another one of those patented smiles.

"So," she responded, trying not to let it warm her.

"That's Margie. She's... quite something."

"She is." That seemed the simplest response. "It was nice of her to invite us."

"She always needs a project. Not that you're... I mean, she might complain about me not sending an engraved response, but she lives for this."

Anne-Marie could tell that was true, so she tried to ignore the part where he'd implied she was a problem in need of fixing, even though she knew it was true. "I need to finish here and get home to cook."

"Oh, sure. I didn't mean to keep you."

She didn't move. He didn't either. She glanced at the notch in his throat, and her skin burned with mortification. Work and stress and gossip made her stupid. She needed to get home.

But when she tried to get away, her cart squawked, and he laughed.

"Hold these." He shoved the beer and cereal at her, and then knelt. He fussed with the troublesome wheel, advancing it with a finger. He dug in the bracket, eventually producing a wadded-up ball of paper.

He pushed the cart, and it rolled down the aisle without a sound.

In spite of herself, she looked down at him, still on his knees, and smiled. "You're wonderful."

The moment she'd said the words, she wanted them back. He wasn't... That was, she hadn't thought to look for the source of the problem there. She'd seen it as intractable. But if she'd looked, she could have fixed it. There was nothing special about him.

What she should have said was, *You're pragmatic. Thank you for fixing my problem, even though I could have handled it.* Yes, that would have been better than wonderful. And more accurate, too.

But her body didn't seem to know that. Other than when he'd lit her cigarettes, they'd never been this close. She could feel him, actually feel the heat from his body. He could reach up and hold her.

Not that he would. But his eyes were bright and focused on her, and his breathing was shallow—as if he were thinking the same thing she was.

This was not aiding her plan to ignore him.

She thrust his groceries at him. "Thank you."

Ignoring the last items on her list, she dashed for the register and from there to her car. She was only shopping in the morning from now on.

CHAPTER SEVEN

Kit tossed the football to an eager Freddie. Now, this, this was easy. Tossing the ball back and forth, no need to search for conversation, no hero worship shining in Freddie's eyes, only purest concentration.

What was hard was not glancing at Freddie's mom once the ball rolled off his fingertips.

Mrs. Smith's kids might like him—and his dog, they *loved* his dog—but she certainly didn't.

The Dunsfords' party was in full swing. Margie's meticulously planned dinner was now in everyone's belly, and most people were in the backyard, enjoying the evening air under the tiki torches.

Rather than chat up his lovely blonde dinner partner—clearly Margie's latest candidate in her campaign to marry Kit off—he'd chosen instead to toss the football with the kids. It was no hardship, truly. He liked Freddie and Lisa—they were smart and polite. Their hero worship of him was somehow more palatable than the rest of America's.

Mrs. Smith didn't like it, though. Or his fixing her cart in the store yesterday, or his saving her from the awkward social situation she'd obviously been in. Her stiff back and rigid jaw had been those of a woman infuriated to be trapped in a conversation.

She'd said he was wonderful and then run as if she'd been frightened by those words. And tonight, she'd ignored him with a force of will he could feel from across the room. They hadn't been seated close, but the one time they'd locked eyes, she'd looked away. He'd tried to the point of rudeness to everyone around him to catch her attention again, but she'd never deigned to give it.

Oh, she was avoiding him all right. Across the lawn, Carruthers was talking her up at the moment. Her shoulders were set unyieldingly against the application of the other man's charm.

But Kit was done rescuing her. He'd smacked his head against the wall of her disdain once too often. He had to quit before he got a concussion.

"Hey, Kit! Catch!"

Kit turned away from Mrs. Smith just in time to catch Freddie's toss. The kid had a good arm, but he needed to work on his control. Maybe in a few years, with some practice—

He'd what? Kit wasn't his father, wouldn't be tossing the ball with him beyond tonight, most likely.

"Go long," he said to Freddie, who ran backwards with an open, eager expression on his face, not even glancing behind him. Because his idol had told him to go long. Nothing bad could possibly happen to him while he was obeying an astronaut.

Kit snapped the ball off his fingers with more force than he'd intended. His gaze followed the ball just long enough to see Freddie catch it to his chest with a grunt, then he was searching out Mrs. Smith again, almost against his will.

Carruthers was raising his hand in slow motion, his eyes slits of calculation even as he wore an innocent smile.

And he set his hand in the small of Mrs. Smith's back.

It was only two fingers there, lingering for half a second at most—a perfectly friendly, unobjectionable touch, but Mrs. Smith did not like it. She never dropped her polite smile, but the edges of it stretched toward the breaking point.

Kit saw red. "Hang on, Freddie," he called. "I'll be right back."

He walked purposefully over to the two of them, putting on a lazy smile as he bore down on them. Carruthers saw him first, his expression slipping.

"Campbell," the other man called to him, an edge behind the words that asked, *What are you doing?*

"Carruthers," he called back, letting his face fall into his "superior officer" expression for half a moment.

Carruthers was a Navy man and below him in rank—he'd take the hint.

But just in case, Kit took that hint and made it a broad suggestion. "Mrs. Smith." He smiled as he always did at her—polite, charming. *Astronaut at your service, ma'am.*

She glared back as she always did. Well, it was either him or Carruthers. She could pick.

"I thought I'd claim that dance you promised me." His gaze flicked to Carruthers. "If this is a good time."

The other man held his gaze for a half a moment—just long enough for Kit to think about pulling rank once more—but then Carruthers lifted his brows.

So there is something there, those brows said.

Hell. He was never going to hear the end of this at work. But given a choice between facing insults at the job or Mrs. Smith's strained smile as she wilted under Carruthers's hand... well, he'd already made that choice, hadn't he?

"Now's fine," Mrs. Smith said, her smile a twist of lemon. She turned away from Carruthers, giving him only her back in farewell. Oh, she must be angry to be so impolite. Kit didn't think he'd ever seen her so put out, at least with someone who wasn't him.

"Shall we?" She headed for the concrete pad other couples were using as a dance floor without waiting for him.

Carruthers sent him a smirk that said, *Good luck.*

He'd need it.

Joey Dee was singing about the twist on the hi-fi. Kit caught Anne-Marie at the waist and took her hand. She was stiff in his arms but close, so close. She only came up to his shoulder, and she was carefully looking at their feet moving together so that all he could see was the brightness of her hair. And the vivid green of her silk sheath dress, the fabric rucking around her hips, the scalloped neckline revealing love-ly, freckled flesh.

He reminded himself to breathe.

"I'm sorry about him," he offered after a few beats. Better if Carruthers himself would apologize, but Kit's remorse would have to do for now.

Her hand tightened on his. The wrong words. He was always saying the wrong thing to her, although he never could figure out how he was off.

"He wasn't doing anything."

Kit supposed he really hadn't. But Carruthers had set his hand at her back, made her distinctly uncom-fortable, and yet she excused him—while Kit was nothing but polite, solicitous, helpful with her—hell, he was trying his damnedest not to think about her hips swishing in that silk—and got sullenness.

"Have I done something wrong?" He said it gently, even as his heart began to race. He'd apologized for the pass, hadn't attempted anything like it since. What if it wasn't anything he'd done, just a general, inexplicable aversion?

He'd never been the object of a woman's disgust before—quite the opposite. And to have such a thing turned on him by a woman he was attracted to? Hell, one that he admired?

Self-loathing was a bitterly new taste for him.

She slowed at his question, but not stiffly. More… consideringly.

"It's not you," she said, although it sounded as if it really were him.

She said nothing more, but they moved easier together than they had at first. Whether because she was less stiff or they were learning each other's cues, he couldn't say.

"Look," he went on, "I like your kids. Your kids love Bucky. But we're neighbors. And if you think I'm not being a good neighbor…"

She sighed and looked up at the stars. He was reminded of the times they'd sat together in dark, gazing at the night sky above them, him reaching out a hand to light her cigarette.

But this was different. He held her to him—no need for the excuse of a cigarette to reach across the space between them. He had only to slide his arm deeper around her waist and there would be no space between them at all.

Perhaps that was the problem. Perhaps he hadn't been able to hide his continuing attraction behind politeness. Which was why it annoyed her.

"When I left Doug," she began, "everyone was horrified."

He leaned in to catch her words, her perfume touching his nose. It was powdery and light—it seemed to float off her skin.

"It was expected that without a husband, I would fail. At everything. As if without a husband, I would stop functioning."

"Ah." It began to make sense, her reluctant acceptance of his help, her pinched reaction whenever he tried to rescue her from distress.

"I needed to prove that I could do things. That leaving Doug was the right thing."

"And I just keep trying to help you?"

"Well, yes. I suppose it's not fair—you are only being polite. But there it is."

They danced a few moments more, the space between them seeming to move with them.

"I know how you feel," he said.

She snorted.

"No, really. Only in perhaps the opposite way." He took a breath, gathered his courage. "They think you'll never succeed. And the same people believe that I can never fail. I can't be a man... I have to be a hero. To all of America."

Their legs brushed together. Because she'd come closer. He swallowed and felt their hips roll in unison.

"I suppose it is harder for you. I don't have all of America watching me," she said.

He shook his head. "No, you have your kids depending on you. I'd rather disappoint America than them."

She ducked her head, her breathing rasping a little too quickly. "They're... do you think they're okay?"

"Better than okay." She looked up at him, and he smiled. "They're great kids. I'm glad you moved in next door." He meant that. Even if she disliked him, knowing her kids made it worth it. "Friends? I swear, I won't offer help, unless you ask." His voice lowered. "And all you have to do is ask. You know that."

She held his gaze, and suddenly the world slowed around them. The music, the other couples, even their movements went to syrup. Her hand in his, her hip brushing against him, almost too slow to be real. And then it dissolved and everything—including his heart—leaped to double time.

It was the cousin to what he'd said to her before, but the reaction between them this time was completely different. Humid, rather than dry. Hot, rather than chilled.

Did she—

"Friends," she said firmly, her smile certain. No hint of regret there.

He kept smiling, trying to keep his disappointment in.

Friends was good. Friends was enough. They were neighbors, he liked her kids. Of course, he'd never actually been friends with a woman before, and kids usually made him itchy. But there was a first time for everything.

"Friends," he agreed.

Nothing more.

But nothing less.

Anne-Marie could feel the word between them: *friends*. Absolutely they were. And friends was a good thing—so why did the label feel so severe? Why did she feel rebuffed?

The song ended, and they stopped moving. Kit didn't release her, though, and she didn't pull away. His face was half lit, his mouth masked by shadow while his eyes caught the light. He stared at her with a look aflame with such quiet intensity it might have been rocket fuel.

She started to say something, but instead she swallowed and looked away at the party around them.

Some other couple giggled across the patio. Someone shuffled with records at the stereo. The children were playing around the dark lawn. But all these things were outside the bubble surrounding her and Kit.

The record needle touched down and the speakers crackled. Ezio Pinza came on, singing about a party much like this one, about love and enchantment and other silliness. Kit pulled her closer and his hip brushed hers as he began to move again.

"Friends dance more than once."

And she followed his lead—but only to be polite. They'd just established they were friends. She didn't want to dance with him again. They didn't fit. Without craning her neck, she stood as high as his collar, which was unbuttoned. He'd been wearing a tie and a jacket earlier, when she'd tried so hard not to watch the blonde he'd been sitting with. The blonde blinked so much, Anne-Marie had almost worried the other woman was going to strain her eyelids. Almost.

He'd disposed of the jacket and tie somewhere, maybe when he'd been playing with Freddie, which had been sweet.

Regardless, they couldn't really dance together. He smothered her. When he'd lit her cigarettes in the dark or jogged down the street, she couldn't appreciate his size relative to hers, but up close he was big and manly and tall. He made her feel childish and tiny. She hated that.

But from down here, she could smell his aftershave, something spicy she could almost feel in the back of her throat. She closed her eyes and inhaled.

And missed a step and crashed into him.

Their pelvises bumped and her nose pressed into that notch at the base of his neck. His arms came around her, pulling her tight against him. She trembled.

"Whoa there. I got you." He whispered the words against the shell of her ear and she felt them straight down her spine, where they pooled and ignited. "You okay?"

What she was was kissing his neck. Not kissing, but she didn't know what else to call it when her mouth was pressed against him. She opened her mouth to answer and her lips brushed over his skin. She would have sworn he shivered under her, and his hand definitely tightened on her hip.

Which was ridiculous. She'd tripped. She pulled back and he released her, putting the normal amount of space between them. After a second, they both realized they weren't moving and Kit began leading again.

"I'm sorry. I guess I'm out of practice." She said the words to the darkness around his head—not to him.

She couldn't meet his gaze, not when she'd just... tasted him. "Or perhaps I was never a good dancer."

"Perhaps you've been dancing with the wrong partner."

She scoffed. She had been, but that wasn't the point. Kit was no more right for her than Doug. "Perhaps I shouldn't dance at all."

"Now that would be a crime."

The air between them fairly buzzed. She was aware of her body, of his fingers digging into her waist, of the fall of her feet on the patio, of the heaviness of her breasts. She felt bound by those things, and restless at the same time. She couldn't look him in the eye. She absolutely couldn't look at his neck.

But she couldn't look away, precisely. She stared at the bits of light that flashed on his hair.

She shouldn't have told him the truth—not during those nights in the dark together, and not here. It made this responsiveness, this attraction, worse. No, she noticed him because of his kindness. His fame. Or because of her loneliness. Their proximity. Nothing more.

The song went on. So did their silence.

She resettled her hand on his shoulder. It was a big shoulder, but not god-like. Just solid. She focused on the music, the predictable sway of their bodies. Not of course on his body, but on the steps. They weren't too close. They were merely dancing.

At last Anne-Marie could feel the blush recede from her cheeks. She'd fallen into him. It was fine. She shook her head and looked at him. He'd composed himself and appeared normal—handsome, with his charming façade in place.

"It was sweet of you to throw the ball with Freddie." She needed small talk as distraction.

"My pleasure. He's talented."

"He's a lot of things. But for the astronaut next door to play with him? I doubt you know what that means."

He shrugged, all nonchalance. "I can guess. But it's not an imposition."

She sincerely doubted that was true. She'd rarely met a man who loved his job and hated its strictures as much as Kit. But she was done pushing him. If he wanted to say the adoration of children, or the nation, didn't bother him, who was she to say it did? Polite lies were fine for the two of them, even if they had acknowledged that they were lies.

She went back to staring into the dark and moving out of routine. There, she was safe and composed.

After an eternity, the song ended—the enchanted evening having finally come to an end and reality having set in even for Ezio Pinza—and she sprang away from Kit before the final chord had finished reverberating. "Thank you for the, uh, well both of the danc-es."

He shrugged. "If Carruthers bothers you again, just whistle."

"You'll be there?"

"Something like that."

He smiled down at her, and she had to whirl on her heel and put space between them. Kit was many things. Playboy. Knight in shining armor. Man. None of those were any good for her. They weren't why she'd come to this party, and they weren't what she needed.

She weaved through the people and found Lisa laughing with Sherry Dunsford. "Are you having a good time, honey?"

"Oh yes. Do we have to go home?"

"Pretty soon. It is a school night. Half an hour more."

Lisa opened her mouth to protest, and Anne-Marie steeled herself for what was likely coming. The chil-dren were... asserting their independence of late. Which meant they were adjusting. Oh good.

The tension ground on for a moment, but then Lisa made a pained face and turned on her heel. Sherry towed her away, back toward the other children, and Anne-Marie watched them go. This evening had been worth it for that sight: her kids playing with other children, happy and normal, the divorce only the slightest fissure on the surface.

"I'm glad you came."

Margie Dunsford's voice came from behind her. Anne-Marie turned and smiled—genuinely this time. "Me too. It was very kind of you to invite us."

"You did me a favor. I would have had two extra pounds of meat without you. And"—the other woman dropped her voice to conspiratorial—"I've never seen Kit so attentive."

Anne-Marie swallowed. Of course someone had noticed, though that meant Margie had probably seen Anne-Marie fall into him, too. "Ah, well, he was being indulgent. I'm a clumsy dancer."

Margie cocked her head. "I don't think so."

"He—I—that is…"

"I don't need details." Margie held up a hand. "But I had a suspicion. I'm always happy when I'm right." She suddenly turned her head. "Alan, I said not to throw the ball near the tiki torches."

Alan swiftly reorganized his features from jubilant to chastened.

Margie gave him a long, level look and then turned back to Anne-Marie. "Are you free on Saturday?"

Interesting. Maybe their acquaintance was going to continue beyond a one-party fill-in appearance. "I, uh, think so."

"Good. I host a ladies' bridge night, and we're short a player. How's seven thirty?"

"It's fine."

Anne-Marie might not have meant to move to Lake Glade, and she might not have meant to ingratiate herself to the astronauts and their wives. But since she had, well, she'd much rather have Margie Dunsford on her side. And that meant she'd even play bridge.

Roberta's face alone would make it worth it.

For a few long moments, she and Margie stood together watching the kids play. Freddie and Alan were tossing a ball, the arc between them growing longer with each throw. Lisa and Sherry laughed together between the dormant crepe myrtles.

Anne-Marie exhaled. She could see the future and, for the first time in years, it didn't scare her.

Just then the ball spiked wildly in the air and slammed into the ground inches from one of the torches.

"Boys!" Anne-Marie shouted. "Careful."

"Some people just can't handle limits," Margie muttered. And as she marched away to lecture the kids about fire hazards, Anne-Marie could have sworn the other woman muttered "indulgent my foot" under her breath.

Being managed had its downsides.

CHAPTER EIGHT

Kit slowed his feet, pulled from his belly to bring himself back to a walk. He checked his watch as his chest worked like a bellows.

Six miles in forty-five minutes. Not bad.

All the astronauts were required to exercise so many minutes a week, although Kit suspected he was the only one who went above and beyond the requirement. But it wasn't only the requirement sending him out tonight—a certain neighbor of his might have been foremost in his thoughts all day.

He reached up to the spot where his throat met his shoulders, the same place where she'd put her mouth last night. As far and as fast as he'd run tonight, sweat and wind licking at that very spot, none of it had erased the lingering imprint of her.

He set his hands on his hips and shook his head, his heart and lungs working as if he was still running.

That kiss wasn't even a kiss—it had been a complete accident. She only wanted to be friends.

He came in sight of his house then, Bucky racing ahead to the backyard, no doubt to lap at his water bowl for about ten minutes straight.

Kit followed him, rubbing a hand over his sweat-slick, hair-rough chest. He'd taken off his shirt after the first mile, since it was too dark for anyone to see him.

He studied the tips of his toes as he crossed his front yard, the white of the canvas damply green from grass and flecked with mud. He'd have to leave these by the back door to keep from tracking dirt in. Not that there was anyone beside himself to care.

As he came around the side of the house, Bucky barked once. Kit's gaze snapped up from his shoes.

Anne-Marie was there. Watching him. She wore some old trousers, her hair covered with a kerchief, holding a bag of trash in her hand. Her tongue slipped out from between her lips, swiped across them as she looked him up and down.

He couldn't remember when he'd ever seen a woman looking better.

And he was shirtless and stinking from a run. *Way to impress her, Campbell.*

She simply stared, her eyes wide and roaming over him. She was no doubt horrified by his state of undress—but he didn't care. He stalked over to her, took the trash from her unresisting hands, and hauled it to the bin.

They were only friends, but friends took out the garbage for one another. And if she thought this too presumptuous—well, she'd just have to get over it. There was no way in hell he was letting her take out the trash, not when he was nearby. His mother would have a fit if she knew he'd let a lady carry garbage.

He slammed the lid down on the bin a little too hard. There. That gave her plenty of warning to scoot back into the house.

He dusted off his hands and walked back, only to find that she hadn't moved an inch. Her mouth was parted as if she couldn't quite breathe properly, and she was frowning.

He sighed. If she kept looking like that, he might have to kiss her back to life. And they were only friends.

"Ma'am." He nodded in her direction, preparing to beat a retreat.

But her hands snaked out toward him and then—

Mother of God.

Her fingers snuck beneath the waistband of his shorts and she tugged him toward her. He wasn't wearing any briefs, and the tips of her fingers were dangerously close to his cock. So of course, the damn thing had to stiffen and inch even closer to those trespassing fingers.

She rolled up onto her toes and set her mouth against his.

This was no accident. This was heat and tongue and… moans? Hell, he was moaning. He'd imagined kissing her, but having her lips pressed against his, her tongue in his mouth… daydreams had nothing on this. He cupped the sweet curves of her bottom and pulled her up to him. Thank God she was light and he spent time in the weight room.

She kept her fingers curled around his waistband, dragging his shorts tight against his balls. Which should have been uncomfortable, but with her devouring him, it was arousing as all get out. Her thighs slid around his waist, her calves hooking around his hips, and he sank his fingers deeper into her ass.

She tasted so good, her tongue tangling with his, and Christ, now she was moaning—

Bucky let out one short, sharp bark, and Kit dropped her.

She released a little grunt as her feet hit the ground.

"Are you okay?" Stupid of him, to drop her like that. And what was Bucky barking about—

"Mooooom! Where are you?"

That. Bucky had finally earned his keep.

Anne-Marie turned for her house. "I'm here," she called back. "I'm coming in now."

Thank God Lisa hadn't come out and caught them. But he wished she'd held off for one more minute of soft, gasping…

Anne-Marie made her way to her own back door, leaving Kit standing halfway between her house and his.

Suddenly she was marching back, her forefinger stabbing the air as she shook it in his face. "We," she sputtered, "we need to talk."

Christ. Was there a man alive who'd ever been happy to hear those words?

He touched his fingers to his forehead in a resigned salute. "Yes, ma'am."

She dropped her finger, nodded sharply, and retreated double time for her house.

Just friends. Kit shook his head. What a load of bull.

Anne-Marie shut the back door with as much quiet finesse as she could manage. The kids were down. Finally. She'd spent twenty minutes pacing in the dark to make sure they were actually asleep. What she didn't need was for them to wake up and look for her, not when she needed to talk to Kit.

Or maybe she was being a coward and had needed to work up the nerve.

She hadn't meant to kiss him. She hadn't even known he was jogging—it wasn't his normal time. Didn't he know he was supposed to keep to his schedule? She'd been doing such a good job ignoring him since the party.

The only thing she had in her defense was that it had been a very bad day. She was close, so close, to finishing with the backlog of airline reservations—or Big Ben, as she'd taken to calling it. She was getting fast at the bookings. Arrogantly so. Sometimes she'd call and book multiple reservations at once. She was always working ahead, finishing her notes for one call while she was on hold with another, flipping through the pile to find a third or fourth... and it had been just fine.

Until it wasn't. Until she'd gotten off somehow and hadn't double-checked herself and had somehow booked seven sets of tickets to the wrong people.

It had taken her all afternoon to set it right, hours when she wasn't doing all the other things she was supposed to be doing. Nervous sweat had run down her back, and tension had built all through her as she tried to make it right. And even now she was worried that she'd missed one, and the Stevenses were going to show up at the airport in a month only to find they had tickets to Portland instead of Paris.

Then she'd come home, only to discover that Freddie had forgotten to take in his science project and Lisa was sullen about something—she wouldn't say what—and to top it off, Anne-Marie had burned the casserole she'd meant to reheat.

She stepped outside, mostly to avoid screaming—not at the children, who'd done nothing wrong, but just near them because she was damn tired and this was damn hard and she damn well didn't like doing it on her own, even if she could.

Which was when Kit had come around the corner. He wasn't wearing a shirt, though she was increasingly convinced he shouldn't ever wear one.

And he'd thrown away the trash for her.

And he'd looked at her like she was beautiful, rather than like she resembled a hobo—which she did.

And she'd wanted just for a moment to see herself like that.

So she'd kissed him.

It was a mistake, of course—even if he tasted like her first drink of water in months. Even if the press of his hands against her body had been precisely right. Even if she'd been so aflame with desire she would have let him ravish her in the yard at twilight... if they hadn't been interrupted.

Because they had been interrupted. Because they would always be interrupted.

And they should be. Her desire wasn't the only factor in her life anymore, and it would never be the most important factor. Freddie and Lisa had to come first.

Whatever was between her and Kit threatened the kids' happiness.

She had to convince him it had been a moment of madness. She'd stolen something for herself, but wisely, she'd put it back before she'd been caught. She was sorry about using him—but their kiss had been a one-time-only engagement.

She pushed off the door and picked her way across their yards. He wasn't on his patio.

With a deep breath, she knocked on his door.

Bucky, ever the vigilant watchdog, nudged the curtain with his nose and barked once, short and joyful, before running off into the house. A minute later, Kit slid the door open.

He was, thankfully, wearing clothing. Athletic sweatpants hung from his hips and a white undershirt pulled tight across his chest, revealing the scored muscles underneath. That was clothing... sort of.

She hadn't changed. Okay, so she'd taken off her kerchief and run a brush through her hair. But that was it—except for freshening up her lipstick. And she might have reapplied her perfume... but women in Texas were expected to do that before they went into their own living rooms, let alone to an astronaut's house.

He ran his gaze over her. He didn't seem to mind her attire. He never seemed to mind anything really, except when Carruthers tried stupidly to flirt with her.

Without a word, though with a smile, he stepped aside to admit her.

She took a deep breath and walked into his den. He hadn't been lying the day they'd met. It was clean, with nary a cracker or errant lampshade in sight. Also missing were pretty blondes, though she might have been more comfortable if they had been there.

She wasn't here to see the house. "Kit, about earlier... I'm sorry."

He gave her a gentle smile. "You think I'm upset that you kissed me?"

"I'm not sure. But I am. Upset, that is."

"And so you're apologizing?"

She buried in her face in her hands. He wasn't helping matters. "I shouldn't have kissed you."

He did laugh then, and she dropped her hands from her eyes and crossed her arms over her chest. It was easier to be annoyed with him than attracted to him. But he evidently didn't agree, as after a moment, the mirth in his eyes darkened into something else entirely.

"Yes, you should have." His voice came out rough, as if it were dragged from some place deep inside him. "You should do it again and again, in fact."

"What? Why?"

He took a step toward her. "Anne-Marie, we're not friends."

"No. No, we're not." Whatever else she might be doing with him, she was done with that pretense. None of the feelings she had toward him were anything so pale as friendly.

"I think about you all the time. Well, you and the stars. You're all bound up together now. You have been for weeks." He paused and swallowed, and then with heartbreaking earnestness, he said, "Have dinner with me."

He'd phrased it as a statement, but she could hear the entreaty. That was what surprised her, made her "What?" come out sharp and baffled.

"I want to take you to dinner. I want to bring you flowers. I want to pursue you. And I want to kiss you."

He took another step toward her, and her stomach went rigid and fluttery at once—which was truly dumb.

"Why? What do you want from me?" she demanded. He made a face. But to underscore her point, she asked, "Do you want to marry me?"

"People date to get to know each other."

"Oh, is that why? Because I haven't already been married once? Let me help you! I'm difficult. And stubborn. And when you bolt, because you probably will, I'll have to see you every day. I can't run away again. If you think the gossip is bad now, imagine how bad it will be once I date an astronaut. Oh, and let's not forget my children. Freddie and Lisa? I believe you've met them. They adore you. And when this affair burns out, when you aren't showing up with flowers for dinner anymore, what do you think that will be like for them?"

His expression went from shocked to solemn. "I would never hurt your kids."

"You wouldn't mean to, but that doesn't mean you wouldn't."

He swallowed and looked away. She suddenly felt bad—she was being awful to him. But she had to take care of her kids.

More gently, she said, "Yes, that's why I'm here—to apologize for kissing you. I'm sorry. And now I'm going."

She started for the door, but he reached out and snaked his hand around her upper arm.

"May I kiss you?" There was the entreaty again.

"Didn't you just hear what I said?"

"Every word. May I kiss you?"

The question, their proximity, his hand on her body: all of it made her burn white hot all over. His eyes skimmed over her, from her neck to her blouse and back to her face. Waiting.

She should say no. She knew it. But the same little part of her that had grabbed him—literally grabbed him—this afternoon cried out: *Take this one thing just for you.*

She nodded, stiff and jerky.

Seconds ground by. Minutes, maybe. She wasn't sure. Then he curved his hand around the nape of her neck and bowed her toward him. Inch by inch, his face swallowed up her peripheral vision until he was all she could see. The scent of his soap overwhelmed her. Anticipation rampaged in her body.

"Kit."

As she exhaled his name, her eyelids drifted shut. And in the dark he kissed her so softly she wasn't sure he had. Until he did again. One brush after another, mouth on mouth, until she sighed.

He released her arm, but only so he could gather her against him. Their heat and bodies melted into one grasping, needy thing. He coaxed her mouth open and stroked inside so gently that she shivered.

He was playful and fierce, tender and powerful all at once. She kept making rough animal noises that should probably embarrass her, but at each gasp, his grip tightened. There was no space between them now.

Indeed, the kiss had dissolved into a full-body thing. Their hips were involved. Their thighs. And his chest. Dear Lord, his chest.

He broke from her mouth, skimming down her neck until he could nip at her collarbone. She gripped his shoulders and tilted her head to make it easier for him.

She'd made one kind of argument, but he was making another. And the clever man didn't even need words. At least not ones in English.

She rubbed herself against him, against the coiled strength of his body and his growing arousal. Her body hummed with wanting.

Why couldn't she take this again?

The crux of the problem was publicity. Freddie and Lisa. Her mother. Everyone in Lake Glade. Heck, everyone in America. If it weren't for them, she and Kit could explore whatever it was they needed to explore. It would still be bad if—when—the affair was over, but they were adults. They could handle it. It wasn't like the present was peachy. No, this attraction was erupting between them. An affair couldn't be any worse.

Maybe she could do this crazy, selfish thing without hurting anyone.

He fumbled with the first button on her blouse and abraded the skin he'd revealed with his chin.

"Kit," she murmured into his hair, "What if there's another way?"

"Mm?" He glanced up: eyes half-lidded, hair tousled, and lips swollen. From her. From them.

"We can't date. It's… we just can't. I don't want to." She took a breath, took the leap. "But we could have an affair."

He blinked for a moment. "We see each other in secret?" he said, clarifying. "Like we do now? Except with…"

"Kissing," she supplied.

"I'm hopeful that's among other things."

Heat blazed through her. Whatever else was true, she wanted all the other things.

She pulled out of his grasp and turned. He'd pulled the drapes back to let her in. With the glare on the glass, she couldn't see the stars. But she knew they were there. The Milky Way. Taurus. All the things she noticed now. Because of him.

Why shouldn't she have something just for her?

Why not?

"Okay," she said, more to herself than to him.

His hands gripped her shoulders lightly and his mouth touched her ear. "Really?"

"Okay," she repeated.

"I asked you for this earlier…"

"You didn't really." And he hadn't. It had been re-flexive. Like some men opened doors without thinking about it, Kit propositioned women.

"I'm sorry about my earlier offer—truly. It was rude. But why now?"

She turned to face him. "Because I want to now."

He tugged her, trying to direct her toward the couch, or perhaps his bedroom.

"I have to get home. The kids… it's been a long day. I can't leave them."

"If we're seeing each other, when can I see you?"

"Are you free on Saturday? My mom was going to come so I could go to Margie's, but maybe they can go to her place"—she swallowed—"for the night."

He smiled, a full devilish smile that set off all sorts of silly feelings in all the soft places in her body. Places that hadn't had the slightest reason to feel silly in, oh, forever.

"I'll be free on Saturday."

"Good."

And with one last quick buss, she bolted before she forgot why she needed to.

CHAPTER NINE

Kit didn't think he'd ever embarked on an affair before.

Dating, yes. Intercourse with a woman... well, yes. But a relationship constructed solely for the purpose of clandestine sex? An affair?

Nope. It all sounded so French.

"So, you and that neighbor of yours?" Carruthers asked.

They were side by side on a bench, waiting for their time in the MASTIF: a spinning rig that simulated how a pilot might feel in space. Reynolds was taking his turn in it while Parsons paced and made notes on a clipboard.

"Yeah?" Kit replied, making it clear Carruthers had better tread carefully.

"I thought you didn't like her."

"I never said that. I told you to stay away from her." Just the memory of Carruthers's hand at her back, the way she'd leaned away from him—it pissed Kit off all over again. Especially now that he'd kissed Anne-Marie. She was having an affair with *him*, not that he could use that information to stop Carruthers here.

"Yeah, but after you ran me off, you danced with her," Carruthers accused. "Twice!"

"So?"

Carruthers raised his eyebrows.

"Jesus, is this a Jane Austen novel?" Kit burst out. "She's just my neighbor."

And the woman I'm about to start an affair with.

A woman he admired, appreciated, who had kids he adored, an entire family he'd never want to harm.

He respected her... but she didn't seem to respect him. In fact, sometimes she didn't even seem to like him.

He was an astronaut. All of America loved him.

Her occasional flashes of disinterest shouldn't bother him. After all, he was no saint when it came to loving and leaving someone—but he was bothered all the same.

Not enough to call things off, though. He'd weather her disinterest in public if it meant he'd have her full attention in his bed, that luscious body unwrapped, red curls across his pillow, and her mouth—sweet Jesus, her mouth—all over him—

Parsons slapped the clipboard against his palm, snapping Kit out of his reverie. "You know, if Reynolds were sitting here," he groused, "he'd be discussing the mission. Not some woman."

"That's because Reynolds is married," Carruthers said. And then under his breath, "Which means his dick is dead, for all intents and purposes."

Parsons snorted and resumed his pacing.

Carruthers was wrong. Joe Reynolds looked at his wife with an expression of wonder—almost as if he were looking at the stars. No, there was nothing dead in how Reynolds felt about his wife.

Kit had meant it when he'd told Anne-Marie he wanted to date her. Between looking at the stars with her, dancing with her, kissing her... something had shifted. He didn't want to make half-hearted passes at her. Or date for a few weeks before parting, like all the rest. He wanted to court her. Wanted to see if things led to marriage. Wanted the whole world to know they were together. And that was the problem—literally the entire world would know.

Kit worked his jaw. "Hey, Carruthers?"

Carruthers grunted in reply.

"That last girl you dated?" He took a deep breath. "Where did she find that photographer again?"

Carruthers rubbed a thumb across his chin. "The bushes outside her bedroom window. Why?"

Because I'm about to have an affair with the divorcee next door.

The divorcee next door. Carruthers probably had that on a bingo card somewhere, right next to the square labeled "ménage a trois."

Carruthers hadn't minded when that girl had left him after the photographer incident. There were always more women waiting in the wings. That was part of being an astronaut.

A few weeks ago, Kit would have said that the women were one of the perks. Not publicly, though.

Because all of America was watching him. They wanted to know everything about him, even down to the brand of underwear he wore.

Kit hated it, but he accepted it as part of the deal. He'd chosen to be an astronaut. That was the price he paid for the chance to see the stars.

Anne-Marie didn't even like the stars.

If he and Anne-Marie dated, she and the kids wouldn't choose such attention for themselves—it would be forced on them. Look at what had happened to Carruthers's girl. Or Margie Dunsford. Margie handled all the attention well, but she had to be on all the time, her and the children. Privacy was a distant country they could no longer even visit.

Did he want even half of what he and the rest of them went through on a daily basis visited on Anne-Marie and the kids?

No. No, that would hurt them. And he never wanted to hurt them.

Anne-Marie was right—an affair was best, with no one exposed, no one hurt. No deeper feelings engaged.

He rubbed between his eyebrows. "No reason," he answered Carruthers. "No reason at all."

Anne-Marie knocked on the Dunsfords' door.

"No trump, spades, hearts, diamonds, clubs," she muttered. She'd located an old copy of Hoyle—a wedding present from a fraternity brother of Doug's—and crammed bridge rules for ten minutes after the kids left with her mom. Maybe repetition would make some of it stick? If not, she was going to pass all night and hope it didn't infuriate her partner too much. Well, she could always throw her cards down and yell *gin rummy*, and they could eject her.

She repeated, "Spades, hearts, diamonds, clubs" several times.

"You're right on time," Margie said as she flung the door open. "Come in."

As she entered the Dunsfords' living room, Anne-Marie nearly gasped. Unless more people were coming, it was going to be an intimate affair.

"I think you met them the other night," Margie was saying, "but if not, Betty Henkins and Frances Reynolds, this is Anne-Marie Smith. The one Kit danced with."

"Twice, wasn't it?" Betty said with a wink. "How do you feel about gimlets?" She was wearing a sapphire-toned sheath that set off her small, delicate features and dark, perfectly coifed hair. She could have stepped off the cover of *Redbook*, but she wielded the cocktail shaker like a weapon and her eyes snapped with verve. Anne-Marie's mom would have tagged her a firecracker.

Anne-Marie liked Betty immediately. "Fine. They're fine."

Actually, a drink or three sounded great—and not only for bridge. Anne-Marie shoved the thought away. If she thought about Kit she'd turn the same color as Betty's lipstick—not a good look on her.

"And she brought a Bundt," Frances said. "How lovely." She was pretty in an entirely different way: stately and patrician, like a blonde Jackie Kennedy. Her black silk Eisenhower jacket was understated in a way that spoke to complete sartorial confidence. At the barbeque, she hadn't even seemed to raise her voice at her children, which couldn't be human.

Anne-Marie handed the cake to the hostess and fumbled with her jacket. No, one minute later, it still didn't make any sense. Margie, Betty, and Frances were famous. And she was playing bridge with them.

She walked over to an empty chair. Dear Lord. There'd been a picture in *Life* from precisely this spot. These women had all been profiled next to their husbands. If ASD ever reached the moon, the implication was that these three would be equally responsible.

Twenty minutes, a gimlet, and thankfully no cards later, Anne-Marie had no doubt this was true. At the very least, if the Soviets did beat us there, these women would know who had failed.

"And then he said that Parsons exploded!" Betty was recounting a story about a recent debriefing meeting. The details were sketchy—though it involved whatever had gone wrong on the recent training exercise and a persnickety engineer named Parsons of whom Betty did a spirited imitation.

Betty was a sketch. Anne-Marie and Margie were ruddy-cheeked from laughter and alcohol. Only Frances was still poised.

"Well," Frances said as the hilarity died down, "Stan Jensen is working them too much, with too much pressure. That's all there is to it."

"We knew it was going to be like this. This push to the moon is hard," Margie said. She was so energetic, so competent—she should be running things.

Sadly, at the party Anne-Marie had recognized Mitch Dunsford's jovial tone and wandering eye. They bore significant resemblance to a colleague of Doug's who couldn't keep his hands off the secretaries, and maybe that explained why Margie had taken to managing other people—and ASD—from afar.

Margie turned those keen eyes to Anne-Marie. "Did Kit say anything? About the exercise?"

"Oh, no. That is, I think you have things wrong. We're just neighbors. He wouldn't take me into his confidence." She shifted a bit. He'd said some things to her that felt like confessions, but it had been the darkness. The stars. Or maybe exhaustion. Nothing to do with her.

Betty regarded Anne-Marie over the rim of her gold-flecked, gold-rimmed glass. "He seemed smitten the other night."

Suddenly the prospect of bids and trumps didn't seem so bad.

Anne-Marie quaffed her second drink and went for stupid. "Did he?"

"Oh yes," Frances said. "Joe even commented on it when we got home. *Down for the count* was his phrase."

The entire astronaut corps was no better than cheerleaders.

"He's a lovely neighbor. He's been very... welcoming." Her cheeks were smoldering now. *Welcoming* was certainly one way to put what Kit had been. Obnoxious, beautiful, seductive, infuriating: all those applied too. She tried not to think about his hands on her body, his mouth on her neck, his thigh between hers.

She failed. Utterly. Incineration did not follow.

The other women watched her—expectant and unconvinced. Several beats passed.

"The kids love him," she finished. Which was half the problem—he could break their hearts more easily than he might hers.

"He enjoys kids," Margie agreed. "And unlike some of his colleagues, I can imagine him as a father."

"What would Carruthers do with a baby? I'd give you even odds he'd put gin in the bottle and call it a White Russian." Betty threw back her head and positively cackled.

Margie didn't join in the mirth. She kept her steady gaze focused on Anne-Marie. "So there's nothing going on with you and Kit?"

"Not a thing." Not a thing except all the things she was going to do with him tonight, and maybe another time too, because having an affair—if it were half as fun as the fantasies she'd been having—might just suit her.

But those things hadn't happened yet, and so it wasn't a lie. Feeling a bit better, Anne-Marie smiled. "Aren't we going to play bridge?"

"Maybe when you come next week… and we ask you about Kit again."

Anne-Marie smiled weakly. Well, at least there would be a next week.

CHAPTER TEN

Thankfully Anne-Marie had walked to Margie's, so she didn't have to worry about driving home. Except she wasn't going home. She swallowed a giggle. It seemed so surreal—that she was going to Kit's for the night. That she'd kissed him. That she was going to kiss him again.

That this was her life.

To top it off, it was balmy for February and clear. The moon was nearly full, and it looked so close. Like she could reach up and press her fingertips into the craters.

She didn't meet anyone on the way. If she had, they'd probably be able to smell the scandal wafting off her. Margie, Betty, and Frances had certainly suspected—though no, they didn't suspect anything close to the truth. They thought what was between her and her famous neighbor was infatuation, not lust.

Despite the other women's trust, Anne-Marie truly was scandalous. Maybe Roberta and the rest of the gossips could sense the truth about her the way you could tell which cantaloupes were ripe: instinct or smell or luck or something. At the very least, if every one was going to keep treating her like a pariah, she was going to enjoy some of the benefits, specifically the ones that brought Kit's mouth into contact with hers. Preferably over and over again.

When she rounded on to Harbor View, she glanced at her house. Everything seemed fine. She picked her way across the side yard and back onto Kit's patio. When she knocked on the door, he quickly slid it open and waited.

This was the part where she should kiss him. Just pop up onto her toes and take the lead. She'd done it before. He'd seemed to know what to do after that. Of course he'd been sweaty and shirtless and irresistible then, but he was pretty much always irresistible.

Right. Absolutely. That was what she was going to do.

Or maybe not.

She brushed past him and into his house. Once there, she wrapped her arms around herself and chafed them a bit.

She wanted this. She did. She was going to take it. Soon.

He leaned against the wall and watched her intently. "Do you want something to drink?"

"No. I had something at Margie's." She'd had several somethings, but the walk had sobered her up—perhaps a bit too much.

"Can I take your coat?" He closed the door. The lock clicked as he engaged it. She swallowed.

She took a deep breath. First things first: clothes. She needed to get those off. She started on the buttons of her coat. Her fingers were clumsy, but at last she'd undone the final one. She loosened it from her shoulders. As she removed the coat, she tried to let go of the nerves coursing through her body along with it. It was a scandalous thing. A selfish thing. And it was okay to want it.

She extended her coat to him, but found she couldn't meet his eye. He was too good-looking. Too manly. Too famous. She looked around him, at his house, lovely as a magazine spread.

"Kit, I..."

Before she could get the words out—whatever words she'd been trying to form—he was across the room and kissing her.

Better. This was so much better.

She wrapped her arms around his neck and leaned into the warm certainty of his mouth, the spicy scent of his aftershave, and the muscular expanse of his chest. She burrowed into him and he brought his hands down, anchoring her against him.

"We have," he whispered, his mouth leaving hers to trail along her jaw, "all night."

She made a breathy affirmative noise and tried to block out all thought. Except for his fingers, digging into her hips so hard it almost hurt. Except for the noises she was making in the back of her throat, which would have sounded needy if Kit hadn't been responding so enthusiastically. Except for her pulse, which was echoing in every part of her body. She hadn't known she could feel her heartbeat in her core.

They kissed until her concerns dispersed. The only thoughts she had now were *yes*. And *again please*. And *just like that*.

They'd stumbled over to an ancient sofa against the back wall. It was covered in bumpy brown, white, and blue plaid wool. She hadn't seen all of his house, but this piece didn't fit. Nobody would photograph it for a magazine.

It reminded her of him, actually. Strong. Old fashioned. At odds with its surroundings. But at the moment when he was toppling her onto it, the sofa was more than fine. It was soft—well, soft enough—and flat, which was all she cared about.

Kit found the first snap on her dress and released it. Anne-Marie exhaled. Then he freed the next and the next. Her neckline resisted and then yielded a few inches. With a grateful mumble, he eased her dress straps down, leaving her slip exposed.

She fought her impulse to cross her arms over her chest, to hide herself from his gaze. Only the fact that her dress kept her confined stopped her. Well, and perhaps the ravenous look on his face.

His eyes shifted back to her face and he brushed some of her hair out of the way. "I want to see you. Is that okay?"

It was—but he was right: she was hesitant. Shy. Unlike herself. Doug had been kind. Sweet, even. But most of her experience was in pitch-dark rooms late at night. They'd shared clothed fumbles, discreet and colorless.

Nothing about Kit was either.

She looked away, shut her eyes, but that was worse. It made her more aware of his body wedged between her thighs, warm and heavy and pulsing.

"It's fine," she whispered.

"Honey, we're going to go so slow."

She cracked an eye. "Not too slow?"

He didn't answer, not with words anyway. He bit her. Her slip and brassiere were in the way, but nonetheless, his teeth closed over her nipple. She shivered.

He released her and then inhaled deeply. "We'll go exactly the right speed."

How like a pilot! But before she could answer, he snaked a hand behind her back and unhooked her brassiere. He pulled her dress down around her waist and then dragged her brassiere straps down her arms. When he eased it out of her slip, her nipples rubbed against the silk and she trembled.

"Beautiful."

Beautiful was such a heavy word, and one that she'd never liked. She wasn't beautiful. At her best, she was pretty, and often not even that. It was the wrong word, and it made her doubt him and this moment.

She wriggled in her slip and attempted to parry. "A dollar twenty-five at Ward's."

He chuckled, but the mirth faded, replaced by something hotter. He ducked his head and sucked her into his mouth. Through the fabric, she could feel his tongue lapping at her nipple. It pebbled instantly and she sighed. He made a sound of approval and kept up his efforts.

When she was panting, he lifted his head and cupped her breast. He molded it, kneaded it, weighed one against the other.

"You're ridiculous," she whispered, but she didn't convince even herself. The breathiness undercut the sarcasm.

He shrugged without any apology, and then he re-applied his mouth.

She arched under him and stretched her arms over her head. She felt taut, strung out, as if only his body kept her anchored. The fabric of the couch raised goose bumps up her arms. He braced an arm across hers and at last tugged her slip down her body, baring her breasts to him.

He muttered an appreciative curse and she pulled against his hold.

He shook his head. "Oh no, I like you like this."

His smile was hungry and she wriggled under it, resisting his grip with some force. He didn't give an inch, but in seriousness she really needed him to turn off the lamp. She had the body of a woman who'd nursed two children. She hadn't known perky in years.

Before she could ask for it, he lowered his head and her eyes snapped shut. She couldn't watch him—it distracted from feeling. The man had a very talented tongue.

She gave herself over to the sensation. She would go wherever he wanted to take her, lights or not. She moved under him. She was jittery. She was needy. Her hips rocked against him, asking for things she couldn't voice. She dug her fingers into his forearm.

He released her arms and began shimmying her slip and dress off. She linked eyes with him and watched him uncover her very real mother's body. She raised her bottom and with a final tug from Kit on her clothing, she was nude. He tossed her clothes aside and stared. His gaze swept over her, top to bottom and bottom to top. He exhaled and put a finger to her chin, tipping her face toward him.

And somehow this was the most intimate bit of all.

He hadn't looked away from her eyes, though a lust-glazed grin settled over his features. She could feel herself coloring everywhere. She grew cold—the kind that burned.

"Have a thing for freckles?" As all jokes did, it revealed the truth.

But Kit didn't bite. Not even in the pleasant way. Not looking away, he trailed a finger down her arm and then across her belly.

"Constellations tell a story. Lines connecting points, making a picture. Your freckles do too. Your body does. Anne-Marie, I like your story."

He didn't look away. He didn't even blink. He meant it. Every word. And looking in his eyes, she felt it.

She nearly shook with need.

"Make love to me."

"Yes, ma'am."

Ever accommodating, he scooped her up and headed across the house. Never mind that she wasn't wearing a stitch and he looked like he'd come from work.

She yelped and threw her arms around his neck. "Where are we going?"

"To my bed."

Well then. That sounded promising. He took her down a hallway. She spied a gold bathroom through one door. He boosted her up on his shoulder while he fumbled with another door.

"I like that painting," she remarked, pointing at a canvas covered with orange and brown squares. "It's very... modern."

"I'll give you the full tour in a—well, in a bit."

He managed to get the door open and he carried her into the dark. He deposited her on a bed the size of Alaska, shooed Bucky out, and closed the door. Then he stalked across the room and flicked on a lamp. His eyes were molten with need.

He reached for the hem of his polo shirt and dragged it over his head. That chest that had ensorcelled her from the first day was even more intriguing now that she knew she could touch it. All those muscles dusted lightly with golden hair.

He was the beautiful one.

When she looked back at his face, he was laughing.

"From now on, I'm taking off my shirt first," he said.

"Is that so?"

"Yes. You get distracted and forget to be self-conscious."

She rolled onto her side. "Let's see if it works with your pants too."

It was a forward thing to say. God, it was forward. But she was naked in the man's bed—she could be forward.

Thankfully, Kit didn't seem bothered. He just reached for his belt. He unhooked it, then released the button on his trousers, and finally slid them and his briefs off.

The thunderstruck thing worked for that, too—for his, uh, member. She opened her mouth and then closed it. Wow.

He crawled onto the bed and over her. "Honey, that's the first time I've seen you speechless."

She reached down and ran her fingers over him. Soft skin over glass—so, so many inches of those contrasts. And so close to her. She linked her fingers around him and repeated the motion as he hissed.

"I may have underestimated you," she whispered.

"Realizing that just now?"

He pushed her down onto the bed. He rubbed his face over her stomach, pulled back, and blew. She shook under the thin, cold stream of air. It was hot and cold. Dark and light. It was him.

"I can't take much more of this. I'm going to start begging."

"Do."

She didn't want to think about how he'd gotten good at this. About how he knew where to touch and where to kiss and where to… jeez, what was he doing now? She'd think about all of that tomorrow.

"Please." Her voice was thick and husky.

Kit kissed her instep. Trailed a finger down the length of her foot. And shook his head.

"Please." Her plea was stronger now, and more vulnerable. Strong in its vulnerability, maybe.

He loomed over her and nipped at her throat. His fingers dove into her hair, held her in place while he kissed her deep and wet and long.

She broke from him. "Please, now, please."

He smiled down at her, the light catching on his hair. "You beg so nicely you make me want to not give in."

She pushed up onto her elbows. "So help me, I will leave."

"We can't have that."

He was up in a flash and fumbling in a drawer. What was he doing? Oh, right! Practicalities. His back was to her, a work of art. He'd found protection and was rolling it in place, all his defined muscles moving in sync. His body was infinitely interesting.

When he turned, a condom was in place. He crawled over her and paused.

"I… you…" He trailed off and kissed her—and that was always acceptable.

When he finally pushed into her, she almost screamed in relief. She had never been so ready. Or maybe it had just never been with Kit before.

He filled her up until there wasn't room for anything else, scarcely for breath or thought.

He rolled those hips—those capable hips that were half responsible for her ending up here—and she could only clutch his back and rise to meet him. He nipped at her neck and murmured warm words into her ear.

"So close, so close," was all she could manage in response.

Then it all dissolved. She gasped his name, lost herself to the tingling relief that she'd needed for a long time. Since she'd first seen him at least, but probably well before that.

He was still pumping into her in firm strokes. She hitched her legs around him, opening herself up. She scored her nails down his spine and watched as his own release claimed him. He shuddered and exhaled.

They stayed like that for a long time, breathing hard. Relaxed and still tense at once. Then he opened his eyes and beamed at her. He'd been inside her—still was, as a matter of fact—but this felt more secret, more shared, than the intercourse had been.

He reached up and began playing with her curls.

"I have fantasies about your hair," he said at last. "It's... you're... beautiful."

And there was that word again.

All she said was, "Thank you. You're..." He was so many things. Beautiful, yes, but also kind. And desirable. And famous. And thoughtful. So many things that even now, even after what they'd shared, she couldn't acknowledge.

She went with, "Heavy."

He rolled off her with a chuckle. He trailed his fingers down her leg and finally, regretfully, released her ankle with a squeeze as he stood.

She watched him wrap the condom in a tissue and fumble for his briefs.

"You want that tour now?"

"Yes, please."

There was nothing less romantic than houses. Surely paintings and lamps would put them back on friendly terms.

CHAPTER ELEVEN

"**K**it! Kit!"

Kit paused at his front door at Freddie's bright, high summons. In a few short years, that brightness might begin to crack as a deeper, more mature voice broke through.

He turned to see Freddie running toward him, Lisa close behind, Bucky chasing the both of them. They looked like they were rushing to greet him from a long day's work—like they might rush toward a father.

He swallowed hard. "Freddie! Lisa!" He put on his astronaut's smile. "What are you two up to?"

Where's your mother? he started to ask, but he bit that back because he wasn't certain he wanted to see Anne-Marie right now.

No, that wasn't true. He did want to see her. He just didn't want her children to watch him try to navigate their first meeting after a night of incredible sex.

"Mom told us to go outside and stop bothering her while she was making dinner," Lisa answered. "We were throwing the ball for Bucky."

"What did you do today?" Freddie demanded.

"Did you take any test runs?" Lisa put in.

He held up his hands as he laughed. "Paperwork. I mostly did paperwork." Their groans made him laugh even harder. "Sorry to disappoint you, but it's not all rockets and glamour."

"Hey! You should come have dinner with us," Freddie shouted.

Kit took a step back, his smile dropping. "I don't know—your mom wasn't expecting me. I can't just invite myself."

They'd agreed to an affair. Not dating. Coming to dinner, even if her kids had invited him—that might be too much intimacy for Anne-Marie. And if the press got wind of it...

"We're inviting you," Lisa said. She caught up his hand. "Come on. Mom always makes too much food and then we have to have leftovers."

Freddie grabbed his other hand. "Yeah, we hate leftovers. Please, please, please."

He wanted to. He wanted to see Anne-Marie, to know whether her eyes would light up or if she'd look away. And if she looked away, he hoped at least that her cheeks would blaze. But he shouldn't.

After he'd shown her the house the other night, she'd left with a quick wave. Almost as if now that the sex was over, she was done. No kiss, no hug, no lingering—just *goodbye*. He could understand why some of the women he'd slept with before had been miffed at his quick escapes after.

In the end, he let the kids drag him to their back door, because it felt good. Good to be greeted by happy kids when he came home from work, good to step into a kitchen filled with the savory scent of pot roast. He could almost pretend that he and Anne-Marie were dating, walking into her house like this.

And the lady herself, wearing an apron, bustling about the kitchen—she was better than good. Dainty, flame-haired, and delectable.

She caught sight of him, her eyes widening. For half a moment, something hot sparked within them. Something that made his skin heat and his mouth go dry. And all he could think of was her expression as she climaxed, a sight he wanted to see again and again—

"Mom, Kit's going to eat dinner with us. Is that okay?"

And that was why he didn't want this first meeting to be in front of the kids.

"Um." Her usual look of consternation came over her, the one that said, *Why don't you just go away?*

But she didn't mean that look. At least, not if her reactions from two nights ago were any indication. No, then she hadn't wanted him an inch away. Not until after, at least.

"I don't mean to impose." He really didn't. He should have given the kids an excuse, pulled his hands free, gone inside to his own empty house—

"It's no problem." She addressed her reply to the salad she was making, her voice carefully neutral.

Great. Now they'd have to stew in the tension all night. Maybe she was right—maybe a secret affair was all they could have.

"Yay!" Freddie shouted as he and Lisa began to hop up and down.

"You two," Anne-Marie ordered, "go wash up."

The kids left, chattering about something at school.

He and Anne-Marie were finally alone. He started to reach for her, but he stopped himself. This wasn't the place for that. He looked around. The table needed to be set.

He began opening cupboards. "Where are the plates?"

"You don't have to—"

He gave her his superior officer look, which quieted her. If he was coming to dinner, he'd damn well do something to help. He wasn't going to make the mistake of asking her if he could, only to have her say no.

"Up here." She tapped a cupboard above her head. He reached up to open it, and she moved slightly away. But only slightly, just enough so that he could arch over her.

He found the edges of the plates solely by touch, hard and cold, while keeping his gaze on the soft, warm line of her neck, her own gaze on her hand resting on the countertop. They breathed together, the moment more potent than the countdown to lift off.

Somehow, once they got close without an audience, the awkwardness evaporated, leaving only acute awareness. Thank God.

He exhaled, and the hair over her ear stirred. The cord of longing between them pulled taut and tugged him toward her. One night hadn't been enough. The longing hadn't abated. If anything, it had intensified.

Were they married, this would be the moment when he kissed her as he'd been wanting to all day—a kiss that said, *God, I'm glad to be home.*

And then it would shift to say, *I can't wait for the kids to go to bed.*

He'd give her that kind of kiss, after the stars rose and the kids were in bed. And then he'd slip out her back door and into his bed—sadly alone tonight.

"Found them," he said softly, pulling down four plates.

"Silverware is here," she said just as softly, pointing to a drawer. But her gaze was hot and sharp as it found his.

"Thank you." He pondered her, wondering if there was time to risk a quick kiss to take the terrible edge off their hunger.

"Freddie," Lisa screeched from down the hall, "don't!"

Nope. Definitely not time.

He filled his hands with silverware and headed for the dining room. The kids came barreling in as he was laying out the forks.

"We'll get the glasses," Lisa told him.

"Where are you sitting, Kit?" Freddie asked. "Mom usually sits here." He pointed to the head of the table.

"I was thinking of that spot." He pointed to the foot.

"Oh, good, then you'll be between me and Freddie," Lisa said.

Anne-Marie came in, holding a steaming platter of pot roast in her hands. "Okay, everyone, sit down." She snuck a nervous, almost guilty, glance at Kit before setting down the platter.

Once they were seated, she reached a hand out to Kit. "Your plate, please."

There was a flutter in her voice, and his stomach fluttered in return as he handed it to her. Their hands were linked by the plate for half a moment, and he suddenly remembered reaching across the distance in the dark to light her cigarette, the gesture only slightly more intimate than the one they were engaged in right now.

He released the plate, but their gazes held. Jesus, she was lovely.

One of the kids rattled something, and the moment was broken.

Anne-Marie jerkily scooped some food onto his plate, passed it back without looking at him, then started to dish out food to the kids.

"How was your day?" he asked.

She stilled as if surprised he'd even ask. "Um, good. Well... fine." She handed Freddie his plate. "And yours?"

"All he did today was paperwork," Lisa said with some disgust. "Can you believe that?"

Anne-Marie began to serve herself as she said, "Considering that my day was mostly paperwork, yes, I can."

They shared a secret, half-second smile as she sat down.

"We had emergency drills at school," Lisa announced. "Tornado, hurricane, bomb..."

"Will that actually save you if the Reds launch their missiles?" Freddie asked. This was pitched to Kit— because he was an expert on the Reds.

"Uh…" Kit caught Anne-Marie's eye. She shrugged. "You've got to follow your teacher's instructions if that does happen."

A deflection from the original question, but he didn't know what else to say. He didn't want to lie and say they'd be fine, but he also didn't want to panic them.

The kids accepted his non-answer though, shooting off to talk about Bucky's latest trick. Perhaps Kit hadn't done so badly then.

He looked down at his plate, up at the kids debating whether to teach the dog to shake or speak, and then across at Anne-Marie. She was watching him evenly right back. It was a weighted silence of stillness and consideration.

She didn't seem uneasy or apprehensive about the scene: her, him, the kids all gathered together in this family dinner. It might be what she said she didn't want, but here in the moment, she seemed content with it.

The warmth spreading through Kit's chest was more than contentment, more than pleasure. Because they were all sitting together, cozy, comfortable, intimate— and Kit couldn't imagine going back to Kraft Dinners with only Bucky as a companion again.

To Tell the Truth blasted in the den, punctuated by the occasional crackle of Freddie and Lisa's laughter. Usually she'd want to know what was so funny, except Kit was helping her with the dishes, which made concentrating on anything else tricky.

"Boss, you missed a spot." Kit tapped the platter and raised a brow. "I expect more from the management."

He clucked his tongue and handed it to her. She glared. It wasn't really a spot, but she dabbed at it with her sponge, rinsed the platter again, and passed it back to him.

"You know, I think the problem isn't with the washing but with the drying."

"That so?" His eyes crinkled as he took the platter and pulled her closer to him along with it. "I guess I just need more practice."

Except that he didn't. He'd cleared the table over her feeble objections and then started helping her wash the dishes with the confidence of a man who did this a lot. As a bachelor she knew he must, but it was like seeing a dog do back flips. She couldn't quite believe it. Her father had never cleared the table or washed a dish.

Doug was marginally better, but he'd almost never been home for dinner. Maybe on the weekends, but even then, they'd usually had people over. Then it had been entertaining, and she'd always handled every detail—including the cleanup.

Having a man for a weekday dinner was odd, even before he set the table and picked up a towel.

She pulled back and handed Kit another glass.

"What's the matter? Am I not doing it right?"

She looked up into his face. "No, you're—" *Perfect.* He was perfect. Except that she stumbled on the word.

"Mom, can Kit help me with my math homework?" Freddie skidded into the kitchen on stockinged feet. "I have about a million fraction problems."

She startled away from Kit, aware for the first time they'd been touching from ankle to hip. "You go," she told Kit. "I just have to wipe down the counters. But thanks. For helping me."

He held her eyes for a long moment. As it had all night, everything around them went indistinct. An inconvenient attraction had buzzed between them from the start—but it was supposed to get better, not worse, now that they were lovers. She didn't like feeling attuned to him.

He gave her a warm nod and followed Freddie out to the den. She dragged a sponge across the counters slowly and listened to the conversation.

Over the din of the television she could hear Kit say, "Hmm, let's look at this one again."

"It isn't right, is it?" Freddie replied, some anxiety in his voice.

Freddie was doing fine in school, but something—
the move, the divorce—had him doubting himself.
He'd always been a thoughtful kid, but the constant
worrying from him was beginning to make her worry.

"Well, how about you tell me what you did?" Kit
sounded warm. Encouraging.

Freddie said, "I multiplied across. The top with the
top and the denominator with the denominator."

Wait, was that correct? It seemed right. She'd been
so good at fractions once, but now she couldn't remember how to multiply them. It just didn't come up
in her daily life. She could cut a recipe by a third or
double it and estimate how much meat she'd need per
guest, but she couldn't describe the details. And how
did you divide fractions? Didn't you have to switch the
top and bottom? Which one was the denominator?
Maybe she was a terrible mother

"Good," Kit said. "But let's look at your answer."

There was a pause. When Freddie answered, the
doubt was gone from his voice. "Oh, I didn't simplify."

An eraser squeaked and then a pencil scratched.
Freddie asked, "How's this?"

"Good job. How about you try those next two?
What about you, Lisa? What are you working on?"

Lisa launched into an explanation about a project on
cursive handwriting that Anne-Marie had never heard

of. She looked at the sponge in her hand and pushed it absently across the counter.

What were she and Kit doing? Was this a good idea?

She'd told him that she didn't want to have a relationship because she didn't want him to hurt the kids unintentionally. But when he'd showed up tonight—which she was confident was the kids' fault—all she'd been able to think about was how happy she was to see him. She'd missed him.

All day her body had hummed, imagining his hands on it. She wanted to see him, to see if he'd blush when he saw her. And he had. She wanted to see if he'd be pleased to see her. And he had been.

But this? Him helping her kids with their homework? It felt familial. It felt like danger. It felt like everything she'd wanted to avoid, but now couldn't deny that she liked.

She stayed in the kitchen, cleaning minute things she didn't do on a typical Monday and listening to the goings-on in the den until it was bedtime.

She strolled in. "Okay, you two," she said to her kids, hoping she sounded normal. "Time for your bath. I'm sure Kit wants to go home." The kids made faces. "Don't start with that. Scoot."

Freddie, in typical fashion, broke first. "Night, Kit!" he called, bolting toward his bedroom.

Lisa started to dash from the room, but then stopped and turned. "Can you come to dinner every night?"

Kit chuckled. "Um, probably not."

"Too bad. Goodnight!" Lisa followed her brother.

Noises filtered down the hall—of the kids jockeying for position in the bathroom, replaying their dinner with an astronaut, and attempting, somewhere in between, to get clean.

She watched the man she'd gone to bed with. And he watched her back. Kit filled up the armchair he'd claimed as if it were his. His den. His house.

The look in his eyes as he considered her was hot and proprietary. She held her ground and his gaze.

"If I didn't say it, the roast was delicious."

She swallowed. "Thank you."

"I'm sorry to have imposed," he said, some of the lust leaving his face. "The kids—"

"I can imagine."

"I'm grateful, though. All that was waiting for me was cold cereal."

In spite of herself, she laughed. "Kit, you're headed to space. You need more nutrition than that."

"I need a lot of things." The lust had returned.

Her cheeks felt febrile. The man was killing her. "I—I'll see you to the door."

She led him to the back, and then, as if she were sleepwalking, she followed him out. Moving with sudden speed, he pinned her against the back of the house and kissed her deeply.

She slid her arms around his neck and kissed him back. Whatever else was true, she loved this part: the weight and heat of him. His hands at her back and sides, his mouth against hers. She went up in flames for him, and if they'd skipped some steps, she didn't remotely care.

She whimpered, and her hands knit into balls in his shirt.

And then he let her go.

"Thank you for dinner." His voice was even, and she was confused. Gently, he disengaged her hands. "Sleep well."

With that, he was gone.

CHAPTER TWELVE

Kit threaded the worm very carefully onto the hook, trying to avoid the barb. He could pilot to the edge of the atmosphere, break air-speed records, and fly a Perseid rocket, but catching a fish without stabbing anyone was serious business. At least it was to Freddie and Lisa Smith, who had never been fishing.

They were at the edge of the dock on the man-made pond, Bucky watching them curiously. He clearly didn't get fishing's appeal.

The entire Smith family had appeared at his door this morning, fishing poles in hand. "These were a gift from my parents," Anne-Marie had explained, a subtle tightness to her jaw. "Apparently, since we have a pond, we should go fishing." She said *fishing* as if being drawn and quartered was higher on her list of desirable things to do.

"Those are nice poles," he told the kids. "Should we go try them out?"

So here they were. On something dangerously close to a *family outing*. Anne-Marie had felt so comfortable with the idea that she'd left the kids with him while she got a picnic together.

He'd done his best not to crow about it. Maybe he was making progress with her.

"There you go, honey." He handed the baited pole back to Lisa. "Now Freddie and I are going to step back, and you can go ahead and cast off."

Lisa gripped the red and white bobber with deadly intent. Those guppies—dear Lord, he hoped there were guppies in there—had better watch out.

He and Freddie backed down the dock, and she let out some line. Then with a flick of her wrist, or maybe two, she sent the hook, worm, and bobber flying over the edge and into the water.

She turned on her toes. "I did it! I did it!"

"Good job. Your turn, buddy."

He repeated the process and a few minutes later, Freddie's hook was soaking in the water.

"What do we do now?" Freddie asked.

The kids were watching him with wide and impressionable eyes.

This was what had always frightened him about children. Well, okay, two things: one, they thought he was perfect. They saw the uniform, or the astronaut helmet, and they thought that was all there was to the business: fame and glory and the American way. They didn't see the part where he'd taken their mom to bed. Where he'd taken a lot of women to bed. Oh hell, he probably shouldn't even be thinking about that in front of children. But they didn't realize he had flaws, was human.

So, two, they cared about what he thought. This question, for example: What do you do while fishing? They didn't know, and whatever Kit—their idol—said, that was going to shape how they thought about fishing for the rest of their lives.

He didn't know how Anne-Marie handled the pressure.

"Well, you eat sandwiches. Your mom should be along with those."

He looked around, but she wasn't anywhere to be seen.

"And you tell stories. And jokes. And you wait."

"For what?" Lisa asked.

Just then, her bobber shot under water.

"For that!" He pointed. "Do you see?"

"You've caught a fish!" Freddie almost dropped his pole he was so overcome.

Kit rested a hand lightly on Lisa's shoulder. The girl was frozen, her eyes bulging out of her face. He squeezed her, and she nodded in acknowledgement. "Now you've got to reel it in."

Lisa went the wrong way at first and advanced more line. Kit could see the bobber, submerged a few inches under water, pull out farther into the pond. But then she turned the reel correctly and the bobber started to slowly edge back toward the dock.

At last she managed to pull the hook out the water. Dangling from it was a six-inch... well, maybe a red fish. He wasn't quite sure.

When the line was about a foot below the floor of the dock, he got down on his knees and hauled it up. The fish danced around, his mouth opening and closing indignantly, the barbed hook poking dangerously from its lip.

"Look at that."

Kit turned at the exclamation to find Anne-Marie standing behind him, a cooler in her hand and a bemused expression on her face.

"Lisa caught dinner," Freddie shouted.

Anne-Marie looked at her son, and she laughed. She closed her eyes and threw her head back and she dissolved. Her shoulders were shaking, her frame vibrating, all the lovely places he wasn't supposed to be thinking about in front of children shimmering with amusement.

It was the most gorgeous thing he'd ever seen.

He'd gotten used to her cold looks and the way she rolled her eyes. Honestly, they aroused the hell out of him now. He knew she didn't mean them. Her ice princess routine was a shield she'd constructed against all the ways in which the world had trampled her. Her frigid demeanor was how she fought back—and he liked that she was a fighter.

But damn, it was good to see her like this too.

When she managed to control herself, she looked back at Kit and wiped her eyes. *Can you believe these two?* her expression said. His heart leapt in his chest exactly like the bobber on Lisa's line. He loved that she was treating him like an ally.

Then she turned her smile on Freddie. "I... Well, it's a bit small to feed us all, don't you think?"

"Can we keep it?" Lisa asked.

Anne-Marie looked at the fish, which was flapping around like a tornado. Then she crouched and said to her daughter, "It looks like a baby to me. Do you think it would be fair for us to take it out of the lake?"

Lisa frowned and stared longingly at the fish. She wanted to keep it. "I suppose not," she said slowly.

"Do you think we should put it back and let it get a bit bigger?"

"Yes." That was dutiful. Anne-Marie had these kids well trained, that was for sure.

"Can you, um, remove it from the hook?" Anne-Marie asked Kit.

"Yes, ma'am."

It took a bit of doing, but he got it off.

"Say goodbye," he instructed Freddie and Lisa.

"Goodbye, fish," the kids chanted.

Lisa's expression tacked on, *I'll be back for you later.*

He stretched out over the dock and released it as gently as he could into the water. The fish shot out of his hand, heading for the bottom as fast as it could. He held there as the fish escaped, with the kids and Anne-Marie watching him.

Was it really this easy, being around children? He didn't have to be a hero here—all he had to do was stick a worm on a line, encourage Lisa to reel it in, then set the fish back into the water. Simple stuff, but it felt heady with a receptive audience.

And with Anne-Marie.

When he was confident the fish was gone, Kit swished his hands around in the water to clean them and rolled to his feet.

When he turned, he found Anne-Marie watching him with heat in her eyes. "Commander Campbell, you move very well for a man of your age." Sass lit her voice.

Before he could respond, she was cracking the cooler open. "It's just a pick-up lunch, I'm afraid, but who wants some?"

She distributed sandwiches and thermoses of juice. While they ate, the kids explained the basic principles of fishing to her.

Once they had finished, the kids went back to their rods and he sat next to Anne-Marie.

"You sure know a lot about catching defenseless be-
ings," she whispered. "Fish, blondes..."

"The girl next door?"

The expression in her eyes was a mix of sweetness
and lust that he felt in every cell in his body.

He should have had an affair long ago. Party girls
like Miss Delancy had their place—the first part of his
life. But since they never stayed around very long, Kit
had never developed jokes with them. Hadn't realized
that could be part of the fun.

Then Anne-Marie winked, actually winked at him,
and it took self-control he didn't know he had not to
tackle her down to the dock.

He resettled and rubbed at his finger, needing a distraction. He had caught himself on a hook at some
point.

"You okay?" she asked, her tone level but concerned.

"Just a scratch."

"Need a bandage?"

"Nah, it'll heal. How's yours?"

"Oh, better. Thanks to you."

For a while they sat in comfortable silence. They listened to the kids arguing about how to best hold a
pole. They watched a gull swoop overhead and fly off.

"You know a lot about fishing," Anne-Marie said at
last.

"My dad taught me."

"He still around?"

"Yeah, he and my mom live in Omaha. He's retired."

"Are they proud of the astronaut in the family?"

He shifted a bit. "Yes. They..."

He paused to find the right words. They were proud, they'd always been proud, but they also wanted him to be satisfied with less. With a house in a city like theirs. A wife. Kids.

He shot a glance at Anne-Marie, who was contentedly watching her children and waiting for the rest of his story.

"They don't understand why I want to see the stars," he said at last.

"They didn't read *A Princess of Mars*?"

He chuckled. "Burroughs was from the library. They were happy I joined the Navy, but the ambition, the things that came later..."

"They don't like it when Jack Paar talks about you on TV?"

"My mom likes that. My dad... he's fairly private."

"Ah."

She understood. After everything that had happened, she was private too. Privacy was the main reason she wouldn't date him. That and her children, of course.

He looked up to see if the kids were listening in, but Freddie and Lisa were too busy discussing the monsters from the picture they'd seen the day before.

"I don't like the publicity, either," he said to Anne-Marie finally. "But it's worth it to me."

She picked at the dock. A tiny silver of wood came off in her hand. She twirled it around and then tossed it into the breeze. "I understand."

There was something sad about how she said it, something wistful and different and he wanted to ask what it was. But before he could, she'd stood up.

"Okay, kids. You've got some homework."

"But I haven't caught anything yet," Freddie whined.

"I did!" Lisa interjected.

"We put it back," her brother replied.

Anne-Marie held up a hand and the arguing ceased. "I promise this isn't the last time you'll go fishing. It's just down the street. And you have rods now."

Reluctantly, the kids packed up to leave. Anne-Marie held herself ramrod straight, her eyes focused on the children and the cooler, everything about her posture ordering him to back off.

Not wanting to make a scene and not wanting the kids to notice that something was off, he did.

"See you, Kit," Freddie said sadly as he followed his mother home.

"Hey, be happy," Kit instructed him. "It's still a good day even when you don't catch anything."

After a second, the kid smiled and Kit trailed them home. Anne-Marie didn't look back at him once the entire time.

CHAPTER THIRTEEN

It started out innocently enough with a phone call from Margie.

"You know the Perseid launch?" the astronaut's wife began as soon as Anne-Marie answered.

"Yes, I've heard of it," Anne-Marie said, trying not to laugh. The launch was the only thing anyone in Lake Glade could talk about—and it was still a week away.

"Well, everyone is good and anxious. So I thought I would host a dinner party tomorrow—"

Because that wouldn't cause additional anxiety? Anne-Marie was grateful Margie couldn't see her rolling her eyes.

"—but Betty thinks it would be better as a progressive dinner party. Now, I'm going to have cocktails and hors d'oeuvres, Frances is going to have the soup, and Betty the dessert."

"No entrée?"

"That's the thing—Kit offered to host the entrée course."

"He did?"

"Oh, yes. I saw him at the market yesterday."

Anne-Marie couldn't imagine Kit volunteering for such a thing. He must have been dragooned.

Margie was still talking. "But you know him—the man can't handle this sort of thing. So can you help him?"

"Me? Help Kit?"

"Well, can you? Will you?"

Anne-Marie hadn't seen him since the fishing expedition, when he'd been so kind with the kids. So kind that he had reminded her why she should avoid him altogether in public and why their affair was a disaster waiting to explode. Ever since then, she had avoided him. She hadn't even allowed herself to watch him jog. She needed to end things now before she got in too deep. Helping him cook and serve a meal in public wasn't a good idea.

But if she said no, she'd lose a valuable ally in Margie. Surely she and Kit could handle one night of friendliness.

"Um, sure."

"Good. He'll have the details!"

And then the other woman hung up, because Margie Dunsford did not have time for salutations or closings, which made sense.

Anne-Marie put a slice of cake in a Tupperware, kicked into her step-ins, and said to the kids, "Who wants to see Kit?"

They couldn't get ready fast enough.

When they pounded on his door two minutes later, Kit answered with a bemused expression. "It's… all the Smiths."

"The kids want to play with Bucky and I brought you some cake." She should have put in some of the roast chicken too—which had turned out well, who knew stuffing it with grapes would work?—but she didn't want him to think she didn't think he could feed himself.

"I'm here on behalf of Margie," she explained.

"About?"

"The dinner you're serving tomorrow."

Kit scratched his cheek. "Yeah, that. She, uh, wanted to do this party—she does them quite a bit—but usually the bachelors can get out of bringing food, only she insisted that we could host my course at your house, seeing as how we were neighbors, and…" He rubbed the back of his neck, looking as discomfited as Anne-Marie felt. "I could use some help."

She scowled at him, and he gave her a sheepish grin in return.

If Margie Dunsford were trying to play matchmaker, there was nothing the two of them could do but keep their heads down and try to avoid getting hit.

They could also end this secret affair, make sure that no one could sense anything between them that might fuel any silliness. She looked up at him, all six foot something of blue-eyed, blond-haired, all-American male sexiness.

Nope. Not quite ready to do that.

She didn't want to hurt Lisa or Freddie, but she also wasn't going to stop seeing him. Not yet anyway.

They turned and watched the kids, who were chasing Bucky in circles. He'd taken the ball and didn't seem to want to return it.

"Do you know how many people are coming?" she asked. She might as well meet her doom head on.

"Not precisely."

"Or what you want to serve?"

"That pot roast sure was good." He gave her a hangdog look, which should have annoyed her but only made her want to laugh.

"You're hopeless! But I will help you fix this—"

"I'll help you pay for the food."

"Of course you will." She sighed. "I have a roast in the freezer I can use. The butcher's probably closed and I've got nothing else handy."

"Thank you. Is there anything I can do?'

She made another face. He'd known how to set a table. How to dry dishes. Maybe he had other talents. "How are you with a knife?"

"I'm a Boy Scout."

Like that meant anything. "Follow me."

Back in her kitchen, she began pulling things out of cabinets and setting them on the counters. "There's a marinated pot roast recipe I've been playing with," she explained. "It's a little more special than what I normally make."

"It doesn't have to be special, it just has to be good."

She glanced around. Certain they were alone, she rested her hand on his chest. "That you think so is adorable."

He reached for her. "Adorable, huh?"

She ducked under his arm. "No flirting, Commander. We have work to do." She tapped a cutting board. "Dice this onion."

He made a face but started chopping.

She pulled the roast from the freezer and set it in a casserole dish. Then she opened the pantry and began pushing things around. "How do you feel about potatoes au gratin as a side?"

"Now you want me to peel potatoes? This is like the Navy—though you're the cutest commanding officer I've ever seen."

She considered pinching him, but decided that would send the wrong message.

"I'll do the potatoes tomorrow. Do you like them?"

"I love 'em."

Somehow, knowing that felt too much. Too intimate. Too close. Which was ridiculous, given how much they'd shared already. The man had been inside her; she should know how he liked his potatoes.

"Mom!" Lisa burst into the kitchen. "Bucky rolled in some mud."

Kit nodded. "Yeah, that sounds like him."

"If you're going to keep playing with Kit's dog—inciting him, more like—you need to take care of him." She turned to Kit. "Do you mind if they bathe him?"

"That'd be great," Kit said.

Lisa flushed with excitement. "Really?"

"Uh-huh. Get some soap from your bathroom and use one of the old towels from the linen closet to dry him after."

The girl shivered with excitement and ran off.

"Please don't get any soap in his eyes. Or his ears!" Kit called after her.

Anne-Marie watched her daughter go with a bright spring in her step. She ought to get the kids a dog. Then they'd stop trying to steal Kit's and she could put some needed distance between her family and their famous neighbor—advice she really should take.

Once Lisa left with dog washing supplies, Anne-Marie went back to trying to fix the meal. She found a large pot in a lower cabinet and poured a bottle of wine and some seasonings into it.

"What are you putting in there?" he asked.

"Oh a bit of this and a bit of that." She added a few cloves. "Just some fixings."

"You won't tell me?"

"Nope. It's a secret."

"Anne-Marie." He said her name with such sincerity she glanced over her shoulder at him. "You can trust me."

She bit her lip and hesitated. Then she turned back to her bowl. "Not telling. You'd fold under Margie's questioning in ninety seconds."

She could feel his gaze on her back, but she ignored it and went back to prepping. After a few beats she could hear him doing the same.

Several minutes later, he asked, "Where do you want these?" When she turned, he gestured to the onions with the knife.

"In here."

"What about the roast?"

She crossed the kitchen and poked at the meat in its white-paper wrapping. "I need to wait for it to thaw, but we've done most of the work. At least what we can do tonight."

In silence, Kit washed the cutting board and the knife. She pulled out a cookbook and pretended to consult it while trying not to watch him.

When he was done, he came to stand beside her.

"This goes to show we're a good team."

She shook her head. "No, this goes to show that I'm good at helping you impress Margie."

He slid his hand into her hair and held her head still. "I want to revisit the question of whether we can date."

"We've explored that question and settled it."

"You settled it. I deferred it. You like some parts of our relationship."

Her face heated, but she wasn't going to let him win so easily. She liked sleeping with him, but sex wasn't everything. It was enough—for now. And soon, they'd part. That was always how this was going to end. That he was pretending otherwise made it both easier and harder.

She pulled away from his grip. "I need to check on the kids."

At the door, she drew a deep breath and composed herself. She was going to find the will to end things with Kit—and soon. She had to.

She pulled the door open. And that was when a sopping-wet Bucky zipped into her house.

"The dog's inside!" Lisa shouted, running past Anne-Marie, the towel in her hand.

Freddie, so soaked his shoes creaked, screamed with laughter and darted in after them.

What was happening in her life? Could she make anything go according to plan?

She whirled around and watched the children run after the dog.

"Can't you control him?" she barked at Kit.

"I can't control anyone," Kit said, his voice deep and low. He brushed past her, his hip touching hers, which wasn't strictly necessary, and joined the conga line through the house. They headed toward the den in the back. Shouts, followed by the clatter of dog claws, indicated they didn't end there.

Bucky shot past her, followed by his entourage.

"Mom! Mom! We're going to get him!" Freddie shouted.

Anne-Marie leaned against the wall, watched the scene, and listened. Her children's laughter floated back to her. There was a crash, followed by a bang, and then a muffled clang, but then the parade came back through.

Dog, kid, kid, astronaut. It was like the start of a joke.

They disappeared into the kitchen. There was a thump, a clatter, and Kit's half-swallowed curses. When the dog led them into the living room this time, he was carrying a package wrapped in white paper. And that was too much.

"Bucky! Sit!" she bellowed.

Against all logic, the dog sat.

She wrenched the roast from his jaws. She turned to face the kids and Kit, who'd all frozen in place. Freddie's hands were on his mouth. Lisa's were on her ears. Kit was trying not to crack up.

"Lisa, please get a mop. Freddie, put the furniture to rights."

Kit stalked across the room and grabbed Bucky's collar. They both had the good sense to look chastened.

"Do I want to know what that is?" He eyed the package.

"The roast. And now"—she glanced at the clock—"the butcher is definitely closed. What am I going to do?" What was she saying? This was both of their problem. "*We.* What are we going to do?"

"Well." Kit paused and mirth lit his eyes. "It's wrapped. He didn't really get his mouth on it."

For ten seconds, Anne-Marie wondered whether he was right. What would Helen Corbitt do? *She wouldn't serve the roast.*

She scowled at him twice as hard for making her consider it. "You're incorrigible."

He turned serious. "I will fix this. Somehow."

She wasn't entirely sure what he was referring to, but despite massive evidence to the contrary, and for reasons she couldn't explain—and didn't want to probe— she trusted him.

She walked him, and his wretched dog, to the door. "Okay, then. I guess I'll see you tomorrow."

He'd done it. He'd fixed it. Anne-Marie was going to be so pleased. When he'd driven over to Dick's, he kept imagining her face. And what she might say. *Oh, Kit! You did it. And you're right: we should tell everyone that we're dating.*

And perhaps in his head, she'd also added a few things about how she'd had a good time last weekend and how wonderful he'd made her feel

Okay, that last part was probably too much to hope for. But the rest of it seemed pretty damn likely.

He knocked on her door and waited.

But sadly, when she answered, she didn't look at him at all.

"What is that?" she asked slowly.

Kit boosted the bird in his hands. Perhaps this hadn't been such a good idea. "It's a turkey. I think an eastern turkey," he ventured in answer.

"Where did you get a turkey? Thanksgiving was months ago."

"I have a friend who hunts. He got this one earlier this week."

"You brought me a wild turkey?"

He'd felt rather clever, thinking to call Dick. But the sharp incredulity in her voice had him worried.

She tapped her fingers against her lips, an expression of deep concentration coming across her face. "Actually, I think this will work." She squared her shoulders. "I can do this." She took the turkey from him.

"Do you need me to help?" He'd enjoyed last night, watching her plan. Watching her work. Watching her.

The kids would likely be around, but he could keep his hands to himself. He could chop things again.

She pursed her lips, as if she knew what he was thinking. "No, I'm going to do this one by myself. You and your dog should stay away—far away. Be back here at five, ready to go," she ordered.

He smiled and snapped off a salute. "Yes, ma'am."

When she rolled her eyes, it was with affection—or maybe he was deluding himself.

He walked over to her house that night, knocked, and, when there was no answer, he tried the door. It was unlocked, and the smell of roast turkey wafting from the kitchen made his mouth water.

"I'm here," he called out. "Are you ready?"

"Just a minute," Anne-Marie called back from somewhere in the house.

"Kit!" Freddie came barreling down the hall, hair slicked back and wearing a button-down shirt with a tie. "Are we taking the T-Bird?"

"No, we'll take your car."

Lisa came out then, looking quite the young lady in heels and a skirt. Not so much like Anne-Marie in her features, but very much like her in her gestures and mannerisms.

"You look very nice," Kit offered to Lisa.

She ducked her head, the grin splitting her face making her look like a little girl again. "Thank you."

And then, Anne-Marie. She was draped in lime green silk, her hair a burst of flame above it, the dress hugging the curves of her breasts and waist before flaring out into a full skirt that swished with each step and caressed her calves.

He searched for a compliment to give her, one that would be appropriate in front of the kids, one that wouldn't tip them off to how badly he wanted to tear that dress off her.

"Nice. You look, uh, nice."

"Kit, is something wrong?" Lisa asked. "Your voice sounds funny."

He cleared his throat. "Nope, just a frog."

"Thank you." Anne-Marie's cheeks went pink as she walked up to him. She held something out to him and dropped it into his hand when he reached for it.

The car keys. Right. What else would it be?

"Anything I should know about your car?" he asked.

"You're an astronaut and a test pilot. I think you can handle a sedan," she replied.

A few weeks ago, he would have focused on the edge in her voice—he would have felt like she was insulting him. But now he knew she was teasing. He was making progress with her.

They all traipsed outside. "Freddie, don't forget to open the door for your sister," Kit reminded him.

"Yes, sir," Freddie answered.

Kit opened the door for Anne-Marie, the silk of her skirts whispering to him as she slid in. His fingers tightened on the cold metal door frame as he contemplated the line of her legs, just before she whisked them into the car.

Just friends. Only an affair.

All of that felt like lies as he shut the door and prepared to drive them all to the Dunsfords' for appetizers.

He kept up a chattering conversation with the kids while trying very hard not to think about Anne-Marie sitting next to him, the scent of her perfume touching his nose, her hands folded in her lap, the neat way she tucked her legs beneath her skirt.

But his attempts at inattention only made things worse, until he felt as if his skin were burning with his efforts to not notice her. Just when he thought he might go up in flames, they arrived.

To be greeted by a pack of photographers.

He stopped the car, but left it running. *Shit.* He should have expected this—the press always wanted pictures—but the thought of shoving Anne-Marie and the kids in front of all this...

"Why are they here?" Anne-Marie hissed.

"The launch," he said slowly. "They want pictures to print in the run up to the launch. *Life* has some exclusive access and, well, everyone loves astronauts."

"My kids will be in every newspaper in America, then?"

She sounded quite displeased.

"Probably just *Life*." As if that made it any better.

"Mom?" Lisa asked uncertainly.

"I can take you home," he offered. He wanted to, wanted to shelter them from this circus. He himself couldn't escape it, but they didn't have to weather it too.

Anne-Marie's expression softened. "It's all right, honey." She faced him. "Is it like this before every launch?"

He nodded. "Margie probably planned for this. She doesn't usually let them in the house, though." A small thing, but maybe it would ease Anne-Marie's mind.

She studied the photographers, snapping away as the Dunsfords posed, when Margie spotted them and waved for them to come over.

"She's seen us," Anne-Marie said absently.

"We can still go." Kit didn't want them in the middle of all this, and Anne-Marie didn't want anyone thinking they were together—the whole thing could end up in disaster.

"No." She set her hand on the door handle and wrenched it open, not even waiting for Kit to open it for her. "I've got a fifteen-pound turkey sitting in my oven that will not go to waste. Come on, kids."

Although it was rude and ungentlemanly, Kit could only stare as she marched toward the photographers, head high, shoulders back, and smile wide, as proud as a sailing ship cutting through the waves.

Lisa and Freddie stared with him.

"Come on, guys," he prodded them. "You heard your mother." And they all followed in her wake.

CHAPTER FOURTEEN

Margie Dunsford had been right. It shouldn't be surprising, of course—she was always right—but this entire crazy scheme was working. Sitting around Betty Henkins's table, eating baked Alaska, the final course of this wandering meal, Anne-Marie could see the astronauts relax.

Joe Reynolds, who was the presumptive favorite to fly the first Perseid mission, was sinking against Frances with a genuine smile on his face. Greg Henkins was mixing drinks in the corner and arguing about the merits of rye with Carruthers—who was so relaxed he'd forgotten to be smarmy. And Kit was sitting with the kids in the kitchen. He'd periodically catch her eye and give her a look so heated she was certain her slip was singed.

Somehow, she'd survived tonight. Margie had trotted her and another neighbor out to the press as friends, and the photographers had seemed to buy it. Everyone had been lovely and welcoming. The turkey had been a big hit. She should be pleased. And relieved. And relaxed. Everyone else was.

Instead, she was restless.

"No, no," Storch was saying across from her, "you're entirely wrong. Doris Day took the pill and then they got the marriage license—"

"And she didn't remember this?" Reynolds replied.

"The pill affected her memory."

"It was Rock Hudson!" Margie shouted from the kitchen.

"I think he faked the license later," Reynolds explained. He turned to her. "What do you think?"

"I didn't see it." She hadn't felt much like romantic comedies lately and she hadn't really had the time.

"But would you remember marrying Rock?" Betty asked.

"I—" She caught Kit's eye across the room. He was worried for her, that this talk of marriage and annulment and scandal might make her uncomfortable.

Except she was fine. This was small talk—and she was superb at that. And these people, or at least their wives, were friendly. They didn't think she was untouchable.

She turned back to Betty and shrugged. "It sounds like it's was Rock's fault—who invents a pill like that anyway?"

"Well now you're making sense!" Margie shouted.

The room dissolved into laughter and shouting, but she was insensitive to it. All she could see was the almost-smile on Kit's mouth. And his eyes—his big blue eyes boring into her, as if he wanted to see her in this moment always.

An affair. This was an affair. This was temporary.

By the next launch, she wouldn't be here. Margie would have given up trying to fix them up. The lust would have burned out and he would have moved on. He'd be here with someone else, and that was… it was fine.

She shook her head vigorously against the image and muttered, "Excuse me"—not that anyone was paying attention.

Up a half-flight of stairs she found the bathroom. She shut the door but didn't bother with the lights. She sagged against the wall.

She'd done foolish things in her life. Things she regretted. Things she'd like to take back. But this one she couldn't even wish undone—and that was the stupidest part about it.

Because it wasn't just an affair, and it wasn't just lust—but all her reasons for wanting it to be were perfectly valid.

Then the door opened, noiselessly. Kit slipped in and closed it, somehow again silently.

"You can't be here," she whispered.

"You're upset."

"Lisa and Freddie are downstairs. The press is downstairs. Most of the most famous people in America are downstairs!" she half-whispered. She felt like pounding on his chest, but she managed to keep her hands to herself.

Kit glanced at the door, suddenly bright and interested. "Elizabeth Taylor is downstairs?"

There was only so much a woman could take. She moved to punch him and he pulled her into his arms. And against all the reasons she shouldn't, she went.

She pressed her face into his neck, not wanting to think. She just wanted to smell his aftershave. To feel his warmth. To taste the salt of his skin. She inhaled and burrowed further into him.

He stroked her back in long, even strokes. "Whatever it is, honey, we'll get through it."

"No, we won't."

He held her for a long moment. She knew why he'd become a test pilot, why ASD thought he'd be a good astronaut: he was as steady as Mount Rushmore. And like a tide feeling the pull of the moon, she wanted to fall into him.

But she couldn't. For the kids, for herself—hell, for him and his career, she couldn't.

She pulled back and he released her.

"You okay?" he asked, brushing some hair off her face.

"Mm." It wasn't really an answer, but he seemed to accept it.

He moved to kiss her and she put up a hand. "I'll muss you."

He gave her a long, slow smile and dropped to his knees.

"What—"

But she couldn't get the question out before he reached for her hem—and that shut her up.

"You've been driving me insane all night," he whispered as he inched her skirt and slip out of the way.

She released an unsteady breath.

"This dress," he went on. "The way you smile. Jeez, your perfume." He'd uncovered her stockings and panties. He leaned into her and inhaled. "Except *you* smell even better." He beamed up at her—but he wasn't done with his uncovering act.

He rolled her clothing up further and nipped at her belly button. "I've missed you." The words were stark and vulnerable. And before she could respond, he kissed her stomach, wet and long. Tongue and teeth and lips, all perfectly applied to make something that should have been strange arousing. Frustrating. Perfect.

She fought back a moan and bowed over him. She hadn't known the world contained what he was doing now. And how poor her life had been without it...

With a shiver, she arched back. She caught her reflection in the mirror. Pleasure transformed her. Lips parted. Eyes half-closed. She was beautiful. With him, she was.

She snapped her eyes closed and made some little noise, mostly out of surprise.

He released her, slid her dress back into place, and stood. He pressed his mouth to her hair once and repeated, "I've missed you."

Then he left. And several seconds later, she dared to open her eyes. She was flushed, but no longer beautiful. She was simply Anne-Marie—freckled and ordinary. Exactly like she'd be when this was inevitably over.

Kit picked up another plate from the dining room table, set it atop the stack in his arms, and made for the kitchen. Anne-Marie hadn't even given a token protest when he'd told her to go help the kids get to bed, that he would start the cleanup.

"Are you in your pajamas yet?" Anne-Marie called to the kids down the hall.

There was a flurry of noise, then a chorus of *yeses*, and… silence.

Anne-Marie's place almost looked worse than his had after his surprise birthday party—who would have guessed astronauts were such a filthy bunch?—but slowly order was being restored with each bit he cleared away. The dishes alone would take an hour. But with two of them, it wouldn't be so bad.

He paused, his dish-filled hand hovering above the sudsy sink. Maybe she didn't want him to help. Maybe she'd shoo him out of the house as soon as the kids were down, happy to finally have an astronaut-free house.

She'd never said what had driven her to the bathroom. He'd done what he could to ease her tension—his own too—and he'd left her with a smile on her face, but sex wouldn't solve all their problems.

He slipped a plate into the water, reached for another. He'd do what he could for now, and if she wanted him to leave, he would.

When he came back into the dining room, Anne-Marie was there, still in her party attire, but wearing an apron and kerchief. She was scrubbing at the sideboard between two chafing dishes with a damp rag, her entire body shaking with the force she was applying. She paused for half a moment as he approached, then scrubbed harder.

He went back to picking up dishes. He knew how to read a keep away sign. "Turkey was good," he offered into the silence between them. "Carruthers couldn't stop talking about it."

They'd all loved her—the other guys, their wives, hell, even the press. She could do this astronaut wife thing. If she wanted.

She didn't look up. "You don't think it was too gamey?"

The clatter of the dirty silverware as he piled it onto a platter was in sharp contrast to the flatness of her tone. "It's wild turkey. It's supposed to be gamey."

"Some people don't like gamey. Maybe everyone was just being polite and secretly hated it." She stopped her scrubbing and dug her knuckles deep into the rag instead.

God, that looked like it hurt, what she was doing to herself.

"Hey." He crossed to her, tugged the rag away from her. She curled her hands into fists. "You did great. Everything was perfect." Gentle and reassuring. And true. It had been perfect. She had been perfect.

She shrugged. "Just doing my patriotic duty."

The flippancy in her voice had him stepping back. "Well, your country thanks you," he tossed off just as flippantly. And a little angrily.

The moment hung between them, heavy and tense. Maybe he should leave. Helping with the dishes wasn't worth it if it only pissed her off more. And honestly, his temper wasn't exactly even at the moment either.

Right as he was about to offer to go, her fists un-curled.

"I'm sorry," she said. "It's just... I got a glimpse to-day of what you have to endure with the press. It wasn't pretty."

He didn't tell her that today the press had been posi-tively gentle. No need to scare her. At least he was get-ting somewhere. "Was that what sent you to the bathroom?" he asked gently.

"Partly," she admitted. "How can you stand it? Just this one evening was more than enough for me."

"Don't worry about me. I can handle it. And I get to go to space. Fair trade, I think."

She tilted her head as she studied him. "And the wives and kids—the ones who get left behind—do they think it's a fair trade?"

He thought on all the funerals he'd attended at Pax River, the widows and kids standing by a flag-draped coffin. An aviator always said that the risk was worth it, that he'd rather die in a plane than in a bed. But no one ever asked the families.

The press asked the astronaut wives all the time how they felt about their men going into space. *Proud, thrilled, happy* was the response that always came back. Exactly the lines they'd been fed by ASD.

"I don't know how they feel," he admitted. "If you want us to stop seeing each other, I understand. Because this—tonight—was only the beginning. We can try to keep our relationship a secret, but the longer this goes on, the more public it will get."

If she said yes, that she wanted to end this... He set his teeth, held his breath. He had to be ready to hear her say that—no matter how badly he didn't want her to.

"I don't think I can," she said softly, finally.

Thank God. It was selfish of him. Hadn't she just said that the exposure of tonight, the prying of the press, was too much for her? But he gave thanks anyway.

"And that scares me," she finished. She fumbled for her pack of cigarettes on the sideboard, tapped one out—and slid it back. "Sorry." She set the pack back, pushed it away from her. "Margie told me you guys are all trying to quit. I shouldn't be smoking around you." She wrapped her arms around herself, tapping her arms with her fingers.

"I'm scared too." A fatal thing for an aviator to admit—but there it was. He felt as if he were in a dead spin with no chance of recovery. The time to hit the eject button was long past.

She looked up at him, eyes wide with surprise, her hands falling to her sides. He waited for her reaction to turn—was she simply surprised? Or appalled?

A careful blankness came over her expression as she walked toward him. And then she was reaching for his hand, linking her fingers with his as she gave him a small, brave smile. "It's okay. We can be scared together. Your secret's safe with me."

He released a breath, squeezed her hand. They stood like that for several moments, hand in hand, the half-cleaned wreckage of the dinner party surrounding them.

"We should finish cleaning," he said finally. But he kept hold of her hand.

"Yes." She didn't let go either.

"Will I see you tonight? Later, at my place?"

"Yes."

CHAPTER FIFTEEN

Twenty minutes after shooing him out of her newly cleaned house, Anne-Marie knocked on Kit's patio door. She was shaking. Not from the cold, though it was. Or from the dark, though clouds masked the stars tonight.

At some point this evening, their relationship had shifted.

They'd left *just* behind. It wasn't just an affair anymore. They weren't just friends. This wasn't just sex.

It was still amorphous. Developing. But it was suddenly more.

Kit opened the door, nude from the waist up, and in spite of everything, she beamed as if it had been days since she'd seen him.

"I can't stay long, I only—" *wanted to see you*, she finished in her head. But instead of saying it, she popped up and pressed her mouth to his.

He pulled her over the threshold, locked the door behind them, began stripping off her clothing, all without breaking the kiss. He wasn't wearing a shirt, so when he shoved her worn blouse to the floor she could press against him, skin to skin.

He should stay like this all the time. Hell, he should go to space without a shirt. They'd surely beat the Soviets that way. Shirtless, muscled Kit was a recipe for world peace.

Which she would tell him as soon as he released her mouth.

He unbuttoned her trousers and she stumbled out of them as he shepherded her toward the couch. They tumbled onto it together. Somehow she ended up beneath him. He reached between them and parted her thighs with a single finger. Moving her panties to the side, he dipped into her core and then brushed up. Again and again he sprinkled feather-light touches over her. She resettled under him, seeking pressure.

"A little lower," she whispered.

Obligingly, he moved a finger, but it wasn't quite… She shifted again.

"Show me," he instructed.

Her eyes flew open. "What?"

"Show me want you want."

She flushed—and not for the right reason. "I, well…"

"I want you in flames here. Show me what you like."

It wasn't that she didn't know what he meant. It wasn't that she didn't know what she wanted. It was that she wasn't sure she could do *that* in front of him.

But this was more. They wanted more. In this room, with this man, maybe she could.

He turned on a lamp and sat back on his heels, watching. She rolled her panties off and tossed them aside, then set a tentative hand on her thigh. She watched him rub a hand over the bulge in his trousers. This, she, was driving him insane. Trying to focus on that, she closed her eyes and complied.

She couldn't think about what she was doing, about how she stroked with her fingers, where and how she was touching herself. She concentrated on the sound of his hand. He groaned and she smiled in response. But then she brushed the right spot and gasped.

He made an appreciative noise and she did it again. Her nerves were electric, her skin fire. She didn't have to school her thoughts anymore. The shame was gone.

Inches away, he was watching her. He wanted to see this—what she liked. If she were brave enough to open her eyes, she'd see him seeing her. As it was, she could hear his hands moving over his own body, and she matched his pace. Deliberate. A bit rough.

Soon her hips were moving in sharp jerks. She was close. She inhaled sharply, so close, and he stilled her wrist.

"That was—you are... hell," he whispered. Then he dropped his head between her thighs and he licked.

She cursed. Something salty that she'd never said in front of anyone. He responded by doing it again. When her knees threatened to snap together involuntarily, he clamped one down against the couch. His other hand snaked in, pressed into her. And with his mouth and his hand, he proceeded to drive her insane.

She didn't watch. She couldn't. She'd read about this in an old copy of Krafft-Ebing that one of her friend's fathers had. It had sounded perverse. Oh, how wrong she'd been.

What was driving her over the edge were the noises. The lapping of his mouth over her flesh. The gasps she made. The bucking of his hips against the couch. This was for her—good God was it for her—but he was close, too. He liked this.

Which was convenient, because he was going to be doing it a lot.

Just then he curled his fingers inside her, touched some hidden place, and she moaned, released, relaxed. He didn't raise his head until the final quake was over.

When she risked opening her eyes at last, she found him leaning against her, watching.

"I have never in my life seen anything I want like I want you."

She swallowed and inhaled. The breath was shallow and now she couldn't seem to get enough oxygen. His eyes were serious. If it was a line, he delivered it with conviction.

Trying to keep things light, she rolled up on her elbow. "The stars? The moon? Even Mars?"

He rose to his feet. "Mars doesn't even come close."

She wanted to disagree. She wanted to argue. She wanted to hide. But she also wanted it to be true.

He shoved his trousers down. He was—if such a thing was possible—more aroused than she'd seen him before. He pulled a condom off a side table and rolled it in place.

"What interesting decor you have," she teased.

"I put it there in an act of desperate hope."

He sat next to her and she moved to straddle him. He nudged against her, asking for entrance, but she didn't move.

Framing her face with his hands, he whispered, "I wanted you before I should have. When I still thought you were married. When you still hated me."

She opened her mouth and shut it. She didn't know what to say, so she shifted and let herself settle onto him. That joining, slick and tender, forestalled debate.

She pitched forward and kissed him, tasting herself on his mouth. She clenched at the thought and his hands on her hips flexed so hard it hurt. So she did it again. She never had known when to quit.

They moved together. He canted forward, running his teeth over her neck, her breasts. She dug her fingers into his shoulders and gloried in the feel of it, of her taking from him. This man, this gentle, polite, brilliant man—and they were groping toward pleasure together with enough force to gutter the furniture.

He pressed his face into her hair. "Jesus, Anne-Marie, I—"

Not wanting him to finish the thought, which sounded like it was going someplace scary, she turned and kissed him. She twisted her hips, sharp and sweet. The pace quickened. Turned more frantic. Her hands balled against his chest and she almost cried out. He absorbed it and slammed into her before finding his own pleasure.

She turned her cheek and leaned against his chest. She listened to his heart. It slowed to a normal rate, but still his arms, banded against her back, didn't loosen. He had her. He would always have her.

After a few minutes, she pushed back. "I need to go. I'm not certain I can make it home, but I need to try."

He lifted her up and set her down while he fussed with the condom. "I know. It's been a long day."

"I'm not certain how I'm going to get up in the morning." She shimmied into her panties and began hunting around for her other clothing. "Oh Lord, do you have anything dangerous to do tomorrow? Are you going to be able to operate on this little sleep?"

He chuckled. "I'll be fine." Then his tone blanched serious. "Thank you."

"For?"

"Dinner. Helping me impress Margie. Opening up."

She blushed as she pulled on her trousers. "Oh, well, you're welcome."

He opened the door. Bucky shot out and a gust of cold air blew in. "Brrr," he said, rubbing his still-bare arms. "It got cold."

"It did." Anne-Marie did enough buttons to keep her blouse closed and then pulled on her coat.

Kit wrapped his arms around her when she attempted to flit out. He pressed his lips to her head. "We'll work out the details, honey. Every one of them. I'm only glad you're willing to try."

She made an affirmative noise and pushed out of his arms. Without looking back she called, "Night!" and dashed home.

CHAPTER SIXTEEN

B eing called in to Parsons's office three days before the launch was a bad sign.

Kit forced himself to be loose-limbed, assured, even though the hard plastic chair was already putting his ass to sleep. But he wouldn't give Parsons the satisfaction of flinching. Or of appearing as anything but supremely confident.

No one else had been called into see Parsons, so he couldn't ask the other guys what was going on. When Parsons went on a tear, the Perseid Six liked to be unified.

Parsons stared back, impassive and blank. He wasn't angry, which should have been good. But he was always angry, so it wasn't good. Basically, where Parsons was concerned, there was no good.

"I should tell you right off," Parsons started, the usual dislike in his voice, "that I don't approve of this decision."

Kit kept silent. He didn't even know what decision Parsons meant, but he wasn't going to admit that. *United front. No cracks.*

And a decision this close to launch? Kit's muscles tensed, as if his chair were shifting.

Parsons steepled his fingers and tapped them together. Still not angry—more pensive. And maybe worried?

What the hell was going on? And was Parsons ever going to say it?

"Reynolds is out," Parsons finally announced.

"What?" Kit came to sharp attention, all of him tingling.

What had happened? For them to pull Reynolds three days before launch, it must have been serious. Reynolds scored highest on all the tests, never made a mistake during drills—he was Parsons's dream astronaut.

Which was why Reynolds was the lead and Kit was backup.

But Reynolds was out.

Kit drew in a jagged breath, adrenaline surging in his veins. Why was Parsons so calm? Given how tightly wound the engineer was, the man ought to be close to exploding. Instead, he was studying Kit with detached disdain.

Perhaps because Kit was the new lead? Kit's lungs tightened. *Parsons hasn't said that you're the lead. Not yet.*

"His kid got appendicitis," Parsons said. "He claims he wants to stay to be with the kid, but his wife must be insisting on it." He shook his head. "To be so god-damned hen-pecked that you'd scuttle a launch for your wife…"

And the wives and kids—the ones who get left behind—do they think it's a fair trade?

Frances Reynolds hadn't thought so. And apparently neither had her husband.

Anne-Marie hadn't sounded as if she thought it a fair trade either.

He couldn't think about her just now. He had to be focused on the mission. Which had now changed.

"Will Robbie be okay?" Kit asked.

"They think so. Which makes Reynolds's decision all the more ridiculous."

Think so didn't sound very encouraging to Kit. Maybe Anne-Marie knew more. He could ask her tonight.

And Parsons still hadn't said who was the new lead.

"I wanted unmarried men from the very beginning," Parsons went on. "Unmarried men have fewer distractions. But PR insisted that married men presented a better image. And now look what's happened!"

What had happened? Was Kit going to space?

The screws digging into his lungs tightened further. If Parsons didn't get to it soon, Kit would just come out and ask him. Screw putting up an impassive front.

Parsons sighed, his fingertips tapping out a staccato beat. "You're the lead. In three days, you're going to be orbiting Earth."

He was going. *He was going.*

"I... I'm happy to serve my country and the mission." Trite, hollow words, nothing like the maelstrom churning within him. But he couldn't very well shout, *I'm going to space, I'm going to space!*

All the training, the drills, his childhood dreams of seeing the stars—he was going. The adrenaline was sharp in his mouth, but he swallowed and steadied himself.

No need to say any more than that.

"Hmm." Parsons wasn't convinced. "You need to be focused. No more sloppiness like with the hatch blowing. Don't think I've forgotten that."

Kit didn't bother to point out once again that it hadn't been his fault. He was going to space. "Yes, sir."

He could afford to kiss Parsons's ass at the moment. He couldn't wait to tell Anne-Marie. And the kids— the kids would be over the moon.

He almost laughed at that. *Over the moon.*

"At least you're not married," Parsons said grudgingly.

Kit froze.

"No, sir." Anne-Marie wasn't his wife. Freddie and Lisa weren't his kids. No matter how it had felt during the dinner party. And after, when he'd held her...

"What about this divorcee?"

Shit. Of course Parsons would hear things—engineers gossiped as much as the rest of them.

How to answer? *She's my neighbor* was true—but she was more than that. They'd agreed last night—they were both reaching for more.

She's my lover. It was true too. They might both be reaching for more, but Kit had come to more all on his own a while ago. And he would have told her so last night if she hadn't stopped him.

Parsons wouldn't understand that. Love couldn't be engineered and was therefore irrelevant to him. Worse than irrelevant: Parsons would see Anne-Marie as a distraction.

He'd just demanded Kit's full focus for the next three days.

Kit ought to deny anything was between them. But after last night—after promising her they'd find a way together—it felt like a betrayal. Of her. Of them.

But if he admitted how he felt for her... he might not be going.

He could reach for her or the moon. Just not both at the same time.

"She's just my neighbor." Saying those words pulled his heart into a jerky rhythm, but he kept on. "Her kids take care of my dog when I'm at the Cape. And that's it." He put a point on those last three words, a warning to Parsons to drop it.

"You're sure?" Parsons's voice was cool.

"Of course." *Liar.*

Parsons didn't look relieved by his admission. What would Kit have to do to convince the man? Besides denying his feelings for Anne-Marie, of course. His fingers tightened on the chair and he wished desperately for a stick of Juicy Fruit. Anything to help work off this tension.

"I need everything to be perfect," Parsons said, gesturing for emphasis. "You, the equipment, the calculations: nothing can fail. The Soviets beat us to space, put a man up before we did. If we lose…"

A chill ran across Kit's skin. It wasn't only his childhood desire to go to space or his relationship with Anne-Marie at stake here. The nation's future was riding on this.

"You don't have to remind me," he said, steady as anything. "I know my duty." Kit had spent his entire adult life serving his country—he knew his duty better than Parsons ever could.

"I hope so. All those rockets that failed, all those cosmonauts triumphant in Red Square—I have nightmares about it." The engineer rubbed a hand over his face as if to erase the echoes of those nightmares.

Kit had never known Parsons cared so much. He'd always had the impression that Parsons considered the space program his personal set of toys and resented the rest of them for touching them. But this confession was almost... human.

"This is everything I've ever wanted," Kit assured him solemnly. "I know you and I have had our differences, but I won't let anything jeopardize this mission."

And if his growing relationship with Anne-Marie was a threat to the mission, then he'd deny it. He'd walk away—for the moment at least. Once he came back, they could take up where they left off. Could move together toward more.

She'd understand. All those confessions of his under the stars—she'd have to understand.

"I'm glad to hear that," Parsons said, displaying the first bit of warmth Kit had seen from him. "But I still would have preferred if Reynolds hadn't backed out."

Kit gave a half-shrug. "Fair enough." No matter what Parsons thought, Reynolds was out.

Kit was going.

"No distractions," Parsons said again. "Nothing but your total focus on this for the next three days."

"You'll have it." His country deserved nothing less

Parsons rose and held out his hand and Kit wiped a sweaty palm on his pants before taking it.

"Congratulations, Commander Campbell. You're going to space. And I'm going to do everything in my power to make sure you come back in one piece."

Someone was crying in the bathroom.

Anne-Marie stood in the corridor at work, one hand resting nervously against the bathroom door. Should she stick her head in and check? Scurry back to her desk and pretend she hadn't heard a thing?

She tried to jiggle the handle, but it wouldn't budge. Locked.

Inside, the muffled crying turned to sobs. That was it: She had to check.

Knocking softly on the door she said, "I'm sorry, but are you okay?"

Whoever was within took a few steps. Telltale heels clicked on the tiles. The crier was a woman, but she didn't answer.

Anne-Marie knocked again. "Can you let me in? We can talk about whatever it is."

The crier blew her nose and paced a bit. Several beats passed. Maybe the crier was waiting for Anne-Marie to go away. How long should she wait? She didn't want to force a confidence. Whoever it was had chosen to cry in the work bathroom—but had probably still expected a measure of privacy.

Finally the lock snapped open and the door pulled back to reveal Roberta.

Well, that was unexpected.

Since she'd started work, Anne-Marie had gotten respectable at her job. She'd finished with the backlog of reservations and made friends with almost everyone. But the blonde office manager remained aloof. Anne-Marie had the sense Roberta continued to gossip about her. She frequently came around the corner into thickets of whispering that abruptly hushed. Her colleagues' eyes would be guilty, and Roberta would smirk. The woman just did not like her.

Anne-Marie supposed most people would feel triumphant about finding Roberta crying in the bathroom. But she didn't feel vindicated or pleased. There was something sad about this.

She stepped inside and closed the door. "Are you okay?" she asked as evenly as she could.

"Yes." Roberta wouldn't look at her. She dabbed at her cheeks with wadded-up toilet paper. The mass was smudged with foundation and blush.

Anne-Marie waited and then asked, "If you're all right, why are you crying in the bathroom?"

Roberta didn't answer. She tossed the paper into the trash and pulled some lipstick out of her purse. She touched up in the mirror and then clicked the tube shut with enough force to rattle Anne-Marie's teeth. Wrenching her purse open, she threw the lipstick inside. Her chin wobbled and she shook herself. At last she turned.

"Why did you leave your husband?" The question was a demand. A plea. An enquiry. As far as Anne-Marie knew, Roberta was unmarried. But whether for herself or someone else, the other woman wanted to know why Anne-Marie had committed that unforgivable sin.

Anne-Marie swallowed and then spit out, "He was unfaithful. As far as I could tell, once I figured it out and put together the pieces, he'd never been faithful. It... it made a sham out of my life and our family. I couldn't put up with it."

"What happened? When you left?"

Anne-Marie crossed her arms over her midsection and leaned against the wall. "No one thought I should leave. Not my friends. Not my parents. No one. It wasn't easy. They thought I would fail—they told me so. But I couldn't stay. I couldn't let the kids grow up in that, thinking that it was normal—that I thought marriage should be like that."

"But you didn't fail." Roberta wasn't asking a question now. Her tone wasn't ironic or mocking. And that

Roberta didn't think Anne-Marie was a failure was a very interesting turn of events.

"No, I didn't," she said with a shake of her head.

Roberta nodded and turned back to the mirror. With practiced sweeps, she started to rearrange her hair, to put every strand back into its proper place.

The tension in the bathroom had eased. Maybe Anne-Marie should start telling the story to everyone she met—or at least all the women.

Anne-Marie waited, knowing Roberta might want to share whatever had driven her in here. Or at least wanting to give her space to do so.

Finally Roberta said, "My sister's husband is an ass."

Anne-Marie snorted but didn't press. Now that the confession had started, it was all going to come out.

"No, he is," the other woman insisted. "He's not faithful. He yells. He... he's an ass."

There were many varieties of asses, Anne-Marie supposed. So she asked, "Does he hit her?"

Doug, whatever his faults, hadn't been violent. She suspected that had he been, the reaction to the divorce might have been different—but she wasn't certain of that. Plenty of women's husbands did hit them and still they were told to stay.

"No, nothing like that." Roberta waved her hand. "Though he has a temper. He's just... *This*"—meaning modern marriage—"is supposed to work because men are supposed to be caretakers. He's just *not*."

Anne-Marie understood. She'd left college. She'd raised children. She'd given dinner parties and made Doug's career the center of her world. And in exchange, he'd ignored her and their vows. He'd turned her sacrifices to rubbish with every hotel room he'd traipsed into with strange women, with every night he'd been late while sleeping with a secretary or kissing someone else's wife at a party.

"What's your sister going to do?" she asked finally.

"I don't know. She doesn't know. And the reason I'm upset is that I can't honestly say whether she should stay or go."

Anne-Marie nodded in sympathy. That was the worst part of all. Without her parents' support—late and hesitant though it was—Anne-Marie's situation would have been a disaster. She wouldn't have had money for a lawyer or a roof over her head. She could have asked Doug for a divorce, but he never would have relented if she hadn't been able to leave. The only reason she'd been able to weather it was her dad's money.

"The world is changing," she offered. "Divorce isn't the bane it once was."

Roberta shook her head. "People are awful to you. I was awful to you."

Anne-Marie certainly couldn't argue with that.

They stood there for a long time, not talking. Roberta powdered her nose. Her eyes were red-rimmed and a touch puffy, but she looked otherwise normal—which was to say icy and lovely. She put her compact back in her purse, smoothed her blue-patterned skirt, and then looked up, locking eyes with Anne-Marie in the mirror.

"I'm sorry."

When Freddie or Lisa had to apologize, Anne-Marie always made them say for what. She also made them promise not to do it again. Roberta notably did neither. But it was a start.

"It's okay." While Anne-Marie might have hoped for friendly colleagues at work, she hadn't expected them. And with the support of Margie Dunsford, it would probably come eventually. When Anne-Marie had some more pieces, everything Roberta had said or done made sense. While Anne-Marie didn't like it, she understood it.

And now her life was better. Terrific actually. She loved her house. She was forming friendships. She knew the kids were happy, rather than just hoping that they were.

And of course there was Kit. If things with them shifted from just an affair to dating and love and marriage... well, she wasn't certain how it would go over.

Would the press revile her or embrace her? Would she be forgiven or denounced?

The other woman crossed the bathroom and reached for the door. Before she opened it, she turned. "I'm glad you left," she said. "More women should leave."

She pulled the handle open and breezed out.

Kit had once told her about how he hated the attention of being an astronaut. How he hated the assumption his life was perfect and the interest everyone had in him. No one thought her life was perfect, but whether she'd known it or not, she'd become a kind of role model when she'd slammed the door on Doug.

She walked over to the sink and washed her hands. Then she glanced up at herself in the mirror. She was sallow in the fluorescent lights. Her hair was positively green in the mirror, her features plain except for her freckles. But she was herself. Her own woman.

Dark bags hung under her eyes—the result of her late night on Saturday with Kit. With him, she'd never be her own woman again. She wouldn't be the woman who left—she'd be the one who'd snagged an astronaut.

She pushed the thought aside and went back to work.

CHAPTER SEVENTEEN

Anne-Marie let herself into her house and dropped her pocketbook on the entry table. What a day. After her conversation with Roberta, she'd processed nine reservations, three of which were international. She didn't want to be vain, but she was something of a travel agent assistant extraordinaire.

She hung her coat in the hall closet and glanced into the living room. It was empty, but muffled shouts echoed from the backyard. When she pushed aside a curtain, she could see her children and her mother talking on the patio with Kit, Bucky at his feet.

She stepped outside to join them, and Freddie gestured at her. "Now will you tell us?" he begged Kit.

What was Kit going to tell them? Oh goodness, was it about... them? On Saturday they'd agreed it wasn't just an affair. She wanted more, and she knew he did too. But maybe they should talk about this first. Once they'd confessed to the kids, there was no going back.

She gave Kit a searching look and he returned it. His jaw was set but he was smiling. The crinkles around his eyes were a bit too tight, like a piecrust about to rip. Maybe he was nervous. She certainly was.

She rubbed her fingers together, trying to release the energy suddenly trapped there. "Hello, everyone. What's Kit going to tell us? Some astronaut secret?"

He nodded slightly and inhaled. "Sort of. I... that is, Joe Reynolds isn't going to fly the mission. Robbie's sick."

"Oh no!" She'd have to call Frances and check in.

"But, you see, well, I am."

"You're what?" she asked, her voice sharper than she'd intended.

"I'm going to space." The tension evaporated from his face. The smile he gave her now was broad and guileless. It wasn't Life's "most charming smile in America"—it was nothing so self-conscious and practiced. Pure, boyish joy had cracked his façade open. He was radiant with it.

For one heady moment, her body bobbed toward him. She wanted to throw herself into his arms and share this with him. Lap it up. Lap him up. Of course she couldn't—at least not in front of her kids and her mother. So she stopped herself.

She shook her head and became aware of them around her, shouting at Kit, excited and happy.

But something else held her back: she had wanted him to tell her family about them. She wanted everyone to know. Kit was going to do this thing—this great and scary thing—and she didn't want to be only his neighbor when he did it. She didn't want to be his... mistress either. She wanted. For the first time in forever, she wanted.

She took a deep breath and pressed a hand to her stomach. All she said was, "Oh."

Kit reached down and ruffled Freddie's hair. The boy vibrated with elation, and a stream of questions and exclamations poured out of his mouth. "What do you think dawn looks like in space? Do you think you can see the tides working? Or the Grand Canyon?"

Lisa bounced on her toes. "And the moon! How big do you think it looks up there? How close will you be to it?"

Kit never lifted his hand from Freddie's head. But quietly, and with greater restraint, he said, "There's more."

"Oh?" Anne-Marie wondered if she'd ever manage anything beyond that one dumb syllable.

"They want me to be totally focused for the next three days until the launch. No... distractions."

Her hand fisted in the fabric of her dress. She didn't answer.

Kit looked up, right at her, and nodded in response to the question she hadn't voiced. That meant her.

His hand passed through Freddie's hair again. He cupped the back of the boy's head in a gesture both tender and possessive. And then his hand fell at his side. "I was wondering if Bucky might be able to stay with you until I'm back."

The kids immediately resumed their happy, affirmative routine. Anne-Marie was aware of her mother congratulating Kit again and then saying something about dinner before heading into the house. Anne-Marie still couldn't bring herself to move or speak.

For several long beats, she and Kit held each other's eyes.

She was a distraction.

These might be Kit's final three days on earth. He might go away never to be seen again. He might blow up on that rocket of his—and he didn't want to see her for the next three days.

She looked away. Blinked. Fought the urge to rub her eyes.

She shouldn't be upset. How silly. She'd wanted to keep things light between them. She'd wanted an affair. And that was what she had gotten.

Oh well, she must have been mistaken Saturday night. It wouldn't be the first time. He didn't want more at all.

She sniffed and looked back up at him. "Of course we'll watch Bucky. Freddie, can you go with..." She trailed off. She couldn't quite say Kit's name just now. When one had affairs with astronauts, well, one had to accept the possibility of being burnt. It was like looking at the sun too long. She felt a bit dizzy.

"—Get the dog's things, will you?" she finished. "Lisa, can you go inside and set the table for your grandmother?"

She turned, needing not to look any more at a certain handsome astronaut—the one who had unexpectedly broken her heart.

"Good luck, Commander Campbell," she called over her shoulder as she darted into the house—where she was absolutely not going to cry in the bathroom.

CHAPTER EIGHTEEN

When Margie opened the door, Anne-Marie said without preamble, "I would like a drink, and I would like for it to be strong."

Margie held out her hand for Anne-Marie's coat and smiled coyly. "Does this have anything to do with a certain someone who headed out for the Cape today?"

Anne-Marie glared but didn't respond. She hadn't known that Kit had left for the Cape. She'd seen him put a suitcase and a duffel bag in his car when she'd glanced—just glanced—out the blinds this morning, but she hadn't been certain he was leaving.

So he'd gone without saying goodbye, had he? Well, she wouldn't want to *distract* him.

She handed her coat to Margie and headed into the living room. Betty was lounging on the couch and flipping through a catalog. The card table was folded against the wall; apparently they'd abandoned even the pretext of bridge—though if it was only the three of them, cards would be difficult.

"No Frances?" Anne-Marie asked, sitting next to Betty and pointing to a picture of an all-white kitchen loaded with built-in accessories. "It's so... clinical."

"Greg would have it covered in footprints in under ninety seconds."

Kit had once told her that Greg Henkins was messy in an absent-minded professor way—and Anne-Marie winced at the memory of happier times, when she was still fooling herself about Kit.

Margie started fussing with things on the bar in the corner. "Robbie's doing better. He came home from the hospital today, but Frances wasn't ready to leave him yet."

"How's Joe doing?" Anne-Marie asked quietly.

As mad as she was at Kit—and more than twenty-four hours later, her rage remained an explosive thing—she was pleased for him. He'd been given the thing he wanted most in the universe. She didn't have personal experience of getting the deepest desire of one's heart, but it had to feel pretty good. However, she was certain he would have preferred if it hadn't come at the expense of his friend. After all, going to space was the deepest desire of Joe Reynolds's heart too.

Margie poured a shot of something into the cocktail shaker with a pharmacist's practiced hand. "I can't tell about Joe. Frances said he's fine, but she also thinks he... Well, she had a lot to say about the ASD brass and their decision-making and family values."

Betty flipped the page and snorted. "If Frances is actually deigning to complain, she must be livid."

Frances did seem above sniping.

Anne-Marie looked away and played with the hem of her skirt. "How did the decision get made?"

"Who knows?" Margie shook the cocktail shaker vigorously and then strained the drink into a lowball glass over fresh ice. "Your guess is as good as mine. They threw darts at a picture of the boys. I called Parsons—"

"You called Parsons?" Betty asked with an incredulous glance.

"He's the only one who knows anything. But of course he wouldn't say. I was lucky to get him on the phone at all." She gave Anne-Marie a level stare. "What did Kit say?"

"He didn't say anything."

Margie crossed the room, dangled the glass in front of Anne-Marie, and then drew it back. "No." She stopped and held the drink too far for Anne-Marie to reach it. "I'm not giving it to you until you tell us what he said."

Betty snapped the catalog shut. "Oh good, I was wondering how we were going to get her to talk."

Margie waved her hand. "I always have a plan."

Anne-Marie glared at them both in turn and lied. "It isn't like that."

"Like what?" Betty canted forward.

"He doesn't tell me about the mission."

Margie set a fist on her hip and frustratingly did not hand over the drink. She waited, brows up, as if Anne-Marie had something to confess. Anne-Marie turned to Betty for help, but Betty mimicked Margie's expression.

They were a united front of well-honed mom shame.

After several seconds, Anne-Marie rolled her eyes. "He said Robbie was sick and Joe was out. He asked the kids to watch Bucky. The end."

Margie extended the glass. "That's a start. You've earned this."

Anne-Marie took it and tossed half the drink down in a single gulp. Her throat seized. She coughed and then wheezed. She had no idea what Margie had made, but it was certainly very strong.

She pounded on her chest a few times and looked from Margie to Betty. Had she earned a reprieve along with her firewater?

"Now that you've scalded the inside of your body—never instruct Margie to make a drink strong—tell us the rest," Betty said.

Apparently not. Anne-Marie played with the glass in her hand. She could of course spill out the entire sordid tale. She'd been mad Kit wanted to tell people, then mad he hadn't, which didn't make sense. She could rectify that wrong.

But it seemed unconsidered to share it without checking in with him, particularly not with two of the biggest gossips at ASD. On the other hand, it had also been unconsidered to make her want him and then to tell her she was a distraction. And Betty and Margie were her friends.

"I mean, I don't know precisely what you think is between us, but if you think it's romantic in nature... you aren't wrong," she said after a few beats.

Margie's mouth quirked. "Oh, we rarely are."

"Kit's not just... he's... Hell, you've seen the man." It was amazing she'd resisted him for as long as she had.

Betty threw her head back and howled with laughter. "Moreover, we've seen how the man looks at you."

"It's a little indecent. You should at least try to hide it from the kids," Margie said.

"Just tell us, is his reputation with women well deserved?" Betty asked.

"Oh, you can tell it is—look at her face."

If their temperature was any indication, Anne-Marie's cheeks were vermilion. But burning though she might be, she was not—she was not—going to talk about Kit's reputation or his manly prowess or anything of that nature with Margie or Betty.

Anne-Marie smothered her face in her free hand. Her friends went on.

"But are his intentions serious, do you think?"

"They must be. He plays with her kids."

"I don't think that necessarily means anything…"

"But in this case?"

"Oh yes. She's got him thinking both short and long-term."

When the giggling died down, Anne-Marie looked up at them and bit her lip. "Please don't tell Mitch or Greg. I don't think there's anything to tell, at any rate."

Margie, appearing to be confident that the juiciest revelations were at an end, headed back to the bar. "Oh, I never tell Mitch anything. He has no sense of discretion—the man is like a sieve. At least he's good at flying things."

"I just…" Anne-Marie trailed off, then took another big sip of her drink. "Kit ended our… our romantic… thing." That was one way of putting it.

"He what?" Betty gasped.

"When he came over yesterday to ask the kids to watch Bucky, he said he didn't have time for distractions before the launch."

Margie slammed the shaker down and gave Anne-Marie a serious look. Apparently they were done joking about sex. "He doesn't."

That wasn't the reaction she'd expected. "But I'm not a distraction," she insisted. She cared for him a lot—far more than she'd known or been willing to admit.

Betty smothered a smile. "Oh, I know, honey. But think about what he's going to do in two days—"

"If the weather is good," Margie interjected.

"—He's going to pilot this rocket, that they're only sort of convinced is safe, around the earth many times. One little mistake and he could blow up."

"Literally." Margie tossed cherries into several glasses.

Betty scooped Anne-Marie's hand up. "Darling, he's in the Navy. And Navy wives, well, they endure worse than being called distractions."

"Korea was still going on when I married Mitch. I went to funerals as a newlywed, wiped the faces of women younger than me who'd lost husbands."

"Before this is over, ASD may bury people."

"You're not helping," Anne-Marie said. She didn't want to think about all the things that could wrong— or, more like, all the things that had to go right. It was easier to be mad at him.

"It's not like the fate of the world is in his hands," Betty went on, "but maybe the future of US-Soviet relations. And certainly the future of ASD."

"Whose side are you on?" The words had an edge, but Anne-Marie followed them with a laugh. Margie and Betty were right, but the look on his face when he'd called her a distraction? Her whole body hurt remembering it. She could either laugh or she could cry—and she'd prefer not to weep in front of them.

"We're on your side," Margie said without hesitation.

"It's just that you haven't had much time to get used to the idea. You've known Kit all of what—a few weeks?" Betty's eyes were empathetic.

Anne-Marie didn't want to think about how fast all of this had happened, so she finished her drink and Margie helpfully set down a tray of fresh, full glasses.

"We need Frances," Betty said to Margie. "She's the perfect Navy wife. She's much better at advice than we are."

"Let's call her!" Margie grabbed a phone from a side table and moved it to the coffee table. She dialed Frances without hesitation. Margie knew the number by heart? How many times a day did she call the astronaut wives? This truly was her vocation: managing everyone, smoothing things over, and explaining. Anne-Marie should have told her eons ago. Maybe Margie could have helped her avoid the entire mess.

"How's Robbie?" Margie asked when Frances answered.

The conversation went on for a while. Anne-Marie turned to Betty when it reached the level of changing bandages and how to tell a good nurse. "Do you think I'm being sensitive?"

Betty shook her head, but her expression was thoughtful. "I don't think Kit has made you feel very confident."

He'd made her feel like she was on fire. He'd made her feel like she wanted to be in a relationship again. But he didn't make her feel anything as solid, as tepid, as confident.

"No," she agreed.

"They"—presumably Betty meant the astronauts— "do need to focus. And whatever you two share, it probably isn't conducive with what he needs to do in the next few days."

Anne-Marie looked away and rubbed at her eyes They were clouded and damp suddenly. Silly eyes.

"So you see," Margie was explaining to Frances, "Anne-Marie feels like Kit thinks she's a distraction... I know, that's what we told her."

"Now I feel foolish," Anne-Marie said to Betty.

Betty shook her head. "You're not."

Margie extended the phone to Anne-Marie. Anne-Marie wasn't certain she wanted to talk to Frances. Actually, she wanted to run home and never see anyone connected to ASD ever again. But she took the receiver anyway.

"I'm so sorry to bother you," she said to Frances.

"Not at all! Honestly, after everything with Robbie and Joe, I'm relieved for the distraction."

Frances was ever gracious.

"Here's what I can tell you, Anne-Marie. I've been married to a pilot since I was nineteen. And if you make it you or the job, the job will win. You have to know that you exist in a universe beyond the job. You're never competing with it."

"You're right," Anne-Marie said. And of course Frances was.

"Kit cares about you," Frances went on. "I know he does. The decisions they have to make about family or ambitions, the pressures... I'm glad Joe didn't have to face this early in his career."

Meaning, presumably, before they'd had children. Because Kit's decision wasn't just about her, it extended to Freddie and Lisa too.

"Is Robbie going to be all right?" she asked softly. Joe Reynolds's decision, after all, was to choose family.

"Yes, he's fine now, thank you," Frances said with a sigh of real relief. "He's eaten about three gallons of ice cream—and proper nutrition is now my main concern about him."

"And how's Joe?"

"Ah, see, you understand this. Joe's... he'll be fine. Being an astronaut wife is about ego and ambition—yours and his. You've got to keep enough of yours and help him find his when he loses it." Several beats passed. "Joe will be fine. And so will you."

"Thank you, Frances."

She handed the phone back to Margie and looked at Betty. "I'm an idiot."

And she was. While she was still mad at Kit, the women had helped her beat it down to a manageable level. He'd given her what she'd wanted. He'd made her no promises. Now she'd have to ask him for what she wanted—which couldn't be any harder than asking him to have an affair with her.

Betty shook her head. "You are nothing of the sort. You're just metamorphosing." As Anne-Marie chuckled, she added, "Hey, this week's homework was all about frogs."

"Are you saying I'm a tadpole?"

"Yes, *ribbit.*" Betty picked up a drink from the tray and handed it to her. "Drink this. And let's figure out what you should wear when Kit comes back."

Margie hung up with Frances and turned to them. "Feeling better?"

"Yes," Anne-Marie said. "If Kit and I, that is, if we—" She wasn't certain how to finish. If she forgave him, if he took her back, if they started dating, if things progressed…

"Get married?" Margie supplied.

Anne-Marie couldn't use the word; she didn't know if she wanted to. But she also knew that if everything became public, that pressure would be there. The kids, her mother, everyone in America would expect them to.

She swallowed. "Would my first marriage threaten Kit's career?"

Margie picked up a glass. "We'll protect you. We'll hush up any gossip."

Betty nodded. "And if things go well with the orbit, ASD won't want to upset Kit. They'll protect you too."

That word *if*. She hated it. But today, if she cared for Kit, if she wanted him, she was going to have to live with it.

"Bottoms up," Margie instructed.

They finished one round and then another, debating whether redheads were restricted to green or if something blue might be nice.

"The main thing is to remind him about your distractions. Maybe wear something that doesn't need a girdle." Betty gestured with her now-empty glass at Anne-Marie, who was fumbling with the buttons on her coat.

Margie nodded. "Just show off those curves and it won't matter which color your choose."

Anne-Marie giggled. "Hmm, I'll let you know what I decide."

"And tomorrow, I'm calling Parsons," Margie said, pulling the door open.

"Whatever for?"

"You need updates during the flight, don't you?"

She hadn't thought of that. She'd assumed she could find out from the news, the radio, about takeoff and landing. But in between? She gurgled, half-agreement and half-nerves.

"I'll take care of it." Margie's words were a vow.

CHAPTER NINETEEN

Kit couldn't move.

That was by design, of course—he was strapped into the seat of the capsule, pinioned like the science experiment he was.

He was strapped into the capsule and the capsule was strapped to a rocket: a neat symmetry. When that countdown hit zero, all that fuel sitting beneath him would ignite and send him hurtling toward the stars.

That was the plan, at least.

He couldn't say that he was nervous. Anxious, perhaps, with a faint twisting in his gut, a slow, deep thrum in his blood. But nothing more than that.

Should he be feeling more? He was about to achieve the dream of a lifetime, after all—to make his nation proud, to stick it to the Soviets. He'd heard a rumor that Gagarin had fallen asleep while waiting for liftoff—and he'd be damned if a Soviet would beat him at coldness or fearlessness.

Kit didn't feel like sleeping. Not that he'd been sleeping much lately anyway.

He'd left Bucky with Anne-Marie and the kids that night—the night he'd told her he couldn't see her for the next three days—and headed for the Cape.

But he'd imagined them, going about their days. Preparing dinner, watching television, playing with Bucky. He missed them. Missed tossing the ball with Freddie, answering Lisa's questions about the rocket design, scratching behind Bucky's ears.

He missed Anne-Marie most of all. The tart things she said. The way she didn't seem to like him until her lust flared to the surface. The floral scent of her skin. The way she flipped her curls out of her eyes. He was distracted by not having his distraction at his side, which had a grim kind of humor to it.

Was Anne-Marie watching the countdown? He knew Freddie and Lisa would be. He wanted to see their faces when the rockets ignited and slowly, slowly left the confines of gravity.

But he was on the rocket.

He'd wanted to spend the last few sleepless nights outside, gazing up at the night sky, but that wasn't possible on the Cape. His every movement had been monitored. He'd considered explaining to his friendly guards, bribing them with beers perhaps, but they wouldn't have seen the romance in it. Or worse, they would have leaked it to the press. And it would have cheapened it to turn it into a promotional thing.

Besides, it would have made him think too much on Anne-Marie. He didn't want to face her hurt, and his own guilt in causing it.

Because she had been hurt. He'd seen it in the way her expression had dropped when he'd said *no distractions*. But with the kids watching and the mission right around the corner, he couldn't explain. He only hoped it wasn't too late when he came back.

If he came back.

He tried unsuccessfully to not think about all the rocket fuel beneath him.

"T minus five minutes."

He wanted to move, to settle himself more securely in the seat. Had they designed this chair for him or the monkey? But he willed himself to be calm. Temperature, respiration, heart rate—all of it was being monitored. No response of his would be hidden from the men in the control room. They knew if he was taking a piss; he didn't want them to see his stress.

But he'd hidden Anne-Marie, hadn't he? Parsons had given no indication that he found Kit's focus lacking in the past three days, even though Kit himself had felt as if it were.

He was going to the stars. He needed to focus on that. The trouble was, after a lifetime of dreaming of a trip to space, there was only blankness now where a thousand fantasies had once been.

This trip would be like nothing he'd ever imagined. It was as if his mind had carved out a space for this mission and was simply waiting for the experience to fill it. The romance of Mars had been replaced by a checklist. The real romance was across the country in a Houston suburb.

"T minus one minute."

Now the countdown began in earnest. The voice in his helmet counted off every second. It seemed to go both too slow and too fast. He couldn't wait for the rocket to lift off. He wasn't ready for the rocket to lift off.

But his heart remained steady, his temperature normal. He was an aviator and an astronaut. Nothing ruffled him.

"Ten, nine, eight..."

He counted off silently with the voice.

And then... *ignition.*

There was an almost deafening burst of noise as the rocket lit, something large and white and blank. Bodily and aurally. Total. Was he moving? Was the rocket lifting like it should?

The clouds began to slip past the window, and he realized that he was. The acceleration was much smoother than in the simulator, so easy as to be almost gliding.

He hadn't suspected that liftoff would be anything but a jerking, shuddering bronc ride. But a man could get used to this.

Up and up and up he went, traveling at speeds men had never seen before, the sky darkening as he rose.

A shudder then—the rocket detaching, having done its job to push him beyond the atmosphere and into the reaches of space. The capsule was now free. And Kit could begin his work piloting it.

His training took over as he fired the thrusters, moving the capsule into position, readying it for the orbits it would make. He looked out the window, intending to use the stars and the Earth below to confirm his position...

And gasped. He'd left Earth while the sun was out, its light obliterating that of the stars. But here—here there was nothing to dim them. They burned bright and cool even in the middle of the day.

He was seeing the stars in the middle of the day. A spill of diamonds in a sea of endless black. He couldn't wait to tell Anne-Marie.

Below, the Earth glowed green and blue and white. He could see the planet's curve, as if it would fit against his palm. He hadn't expected it to be so beautiful.

He noticed then that he was straining slightly against his seat restraints. Straining upward, against all the laws of gravity.

He was weightless.

In the "Vomit Comet," weightlessness wasn't very fun at all. There, he was getting dropped from a very great height, and his stomach knew it.

But this kind of weightlessness was fun. He loosened the restraints and let himself bob upward, a smile splitting his face.

"What's it look like up there?" Parsons radioed. Of course Parsons would cut in right as he was starting to enjoy himself.

Kit looked out the window, at the stars and the planet spinning beneath him. Parsons wanted him to describe this? He wasn't certain he could. But he wanted to capture it, if only to be able to share what he could with Anne-Marie later.

"I can very clearly see the star field," he said carefully, "and can ascertain my position and attitude with it quite easily." Mission Control would need to know that for future flights. "The Earth looks... it looks beautiful."

He wanted to say more, to capture what it really looked like, which was so much more than beautiful. But the words wouldn't come.

Was Anne-Marie listening? He wasn't certain what exactly was being broadcast on the television. If she were, perhaps she'd hear this next and know that he was thinking of her, even now.

"I can see Mars," he said. "It's not as impressive as I expected."

A beat of silence as Parsons digested that. "You can't see Mars," he said irritably.

"Can't I?" Kit smiled, although there was no one but himself to see. "I must be mistaken then."

Parsons's sigh was loud even over the radio. "Start going through your checklist," he ordered.

Kit went back to work, hoping that Anne-Marie had heard his message to her across the thousands of miles between them.

The morning of the launch, Anne-Marie paced some. Then she fretted. And when that failed, she might have pulled out a copy of a certain issue of *Life* and stared at Kit's picture. He looked so competent and at ease. She hoped he felt that way with whatever he was doing right now.

Before she could get truly maudlin, pounding sounded on her front door. She cinched her robe more tightly around herself and looked out the peephole.

What were they doing here? She pulled the door open to reveal Margie, Frances, and Betty. Their arms were filled with food.

"We're so relieved the press aren't outside," Margie said. "Take this." She handed Anne-Marie what appeared to be a frozen lasagna and strode in. "Where's your kitchen?"

"Some trucks drove by earlier," Anne-Marie said, trailing her. "But they left after getting pictures of Kit's house."

The other women began arranging things on the counter.

"And probably yours too," Betty said with a wink.

There had been rumors after the *Life* story about the dinner, but things had quieted down—probably because Kit had ignored her so fastidiously. Hooray.

"Where are Freddie and Lisa?" Margie asked.

"My mom took them to school. I called in sick." While things had been better since her conversation with Roberta, she couldn't handle booking reservations. Not today. She hoped the kids would be okay at school. If something went wrong... she'd need a plan to get them in a hurry. But Margie probably had something worked out.

"The launch is supposed to be in ten minutes, but I..."

"Oh no, it's delayed," Frances said.

"What?"

"Parsons told me. There are clouds, but they're supposed to clear up." Margie was filling the coffee pot. "Do you mind?" she asked, gesturing to what she was doing. She didn't wait for a reply before going on, "He said Kit is focused and calm."

All Anne-Marie could say, quite stupidly, was "Oh."

Frances cupped her cheek. "We'll stay as long as you like. And I think your robe is… charming, but in case the press show up, maybe you should put on a dress."

"I'd make it green," Margie put in.

"Okay." Anne-Marie stood there for a moment, watching them. They were her friends. They were here for her not because they thought she was going to fall apart, but because they cared. How so many things had changed since she'd left Doug.

She headed for her bedroom to put a dress on and some curlers in.

"Who knows," Betty called after her, "when you come back, we might even play some bridge."

They didn't find time for cards. They watched Walter Cronkite, drank three pots of coffee, and ate enough deviled eggs to strangle a horse. And every twenty minutes, Margie called someone named Bill.

"Parsons told me that I couldn't keep bothering him all day," she explained. "So he gave me Bill's direct line."

"But what reason did you give for bothering anyone at all?" Anne-Marie responded.

"Parsons is many things, but he isn't an idiot. I told him I'd be spending the day with you."

After that, there wasn't anything to say but "Oh."

Margie sat on the phone with Bill during liftoff and gave a live report. "The oxygen parameters look good," she said when the final countdown had started.

"What are oxygen parameters?" Betty whispered.

"He's away," Margie interrupted, meaning Kit. "And everything… everything looks good."

Anne-Marie dropped her face to her hands and released the breath she'd been holding.

Frances stroked her back. "We're through the hardest part."

Anne-Marie rubbed her cheeks. Her hands were numb—but it was fine, because she could scarcely feel them on her face. Joy, exhaustion, sleeplessness, and stress were rioting in her. They muddled together into detachment and shock.

"I need… Just give me a moment."

She walked through the house and out onto the patio to stare up at the sky. Right now Kit was somewhere up there. Thousands of miles, tens of thousands of miles away—Bill would probably know. However far it was, he was screaming overhead, strapped to a rocket. He was literally out of this world.

"Please come back," she whispered. "I need to tell you I love you."

Seconds became minutes. Soon she was dazzled by the brightness of the sky and had to look away. A bird sang in a tree. A car drove down the street. Her pulse thundered in her wrists. He was thousands of miles away, but he was coming home. And if she were very lucky, he might just be coming home to her.

Kit watched Australia slip away beneath him, the coastline glowing. An entire continent, ringed with light. For him. Because he was flying past.

It was heady stuff.

He'd thought he'd only want to watch the stars while he was up here. That he'd never be able to look away from those bright jewels.

But after the first orbit, he found himself looking back at Earth more than the stars. There were more clouds than he'd expected, a tattered veil of white encompassing the entire globe. He saw a thunderstorm at one point, lightning flashing throughout the clouds like sparks from a Roman candle.

The ocean was the most beautiful blue from here, a pool of melted sapphires. He could see deserts and forests and mountains striping the continents. He'd passed over Texas twice now, and each time he'd looked very carefully for Houston, wondering if Anne-Marie and the kids were looking up at where he was that very moment.

He couldn't wait to tell them about everything he'd seen. Hawaii was coming up again soon, pass number three. One or two more orbits and he'd come down. Safely, most likely. So far, everything had gone textbook perfect.

"Perseid Two, do you read?" Carruthers's voice broke through Kit's thoughts.

"Roger."

"They're bringing you in early."

The radio was too tinny to let the nuances of Carruthers's tone come through. But to come home early meant something was wrong.

"Why is that?" he asked, keeping his voice level. "I've got at least one more orbit planned."

"Well…" Now the tone came through—Carruthers had some bad news coming. "The heat shield might have come loose."

The heat shield might have come loose?

That wasn't bad news. That was the worst news. Without the heat shield, he was dead. He'd burn to a crisp on reentry. He'd never be able to tell Anne-Marie and the kids about all the wonderful things he'd seen, because he'd be nothing more than ashes in the atmosphere.

He would never have the chance to tell her how much he loved her.

He blew out a breath, stared sightlessly at Hawaii slipping past. "You said might?" he radioed back.

"One of the clamps is signaling as deployed," Carruthers said. "But only the one. The plan is to get into reentry position and hope that the force of deceleration keeps the shield in place. If it really is loose."

Kit wasn't asking the odds on that working. Either it did or it didn't. He had no other choices. Not if he wanted to get back to that beautiful blue and green globe floating beneath him. And a certain red-haired lady he was in love with.

"Am I still firing the retrorockets over California?" he asked.

"Yep."

Which was coming up soon. Over a decade of training took over then, all his aviator instincts coming to the fore until he was nothing but chilled competence. He'd need every bit of his training and skill to survive this. But damn, did he wish he had a stick of Juicy Fruit just now.

"Better get the capsule into position then," he said. "If I'm late, Parsons will have my head."

Carruthers laughed, as Kit had meant him to do.

He got down to business, firing the thrusters and checking his shift in attitude via the instruments. Then double-checking using the horizon and the stars he could see.

"I'm in place," he radioed.

"Just in time."

It was Parsons now, the big man himself come on to help guide him home. It actually reassured Kit—for all his brusqueness, there was no one more invested in the success of the mission than Parsons. Except for maybe Kit himself.

The countdown began, the coast of California appearing outside his window.

"Five, four, three, two, one..."

Kit fired the retrorockets, the force of it shoving him and the capsule back toward the clasp of Earth's gravity. The sense of weightlessness disappeared as the deceleration pushed him against the seat restraints.

Please let the heat shield hold.

The capsule began to oscillate, and he used the controls to hold it steady. If the capsule slipped out of this position, the heat shield might slip too. And then he was done.

Mission Control was squawking in his ear, but he ignored it for the time, concentrating on holding the capsule steady. He checked his attitude out of habit, although if the capsule was off by too much, there was nothing he could do.

The radio went dead.

He'd hit the ionization zone of silence. For the next five minutes, the radio would be useless. He'd known that this would happen, but it was still unnerving. He was completely cut off now, totally isolated. It made the potential loss of the heat shield—his potential death—that much more potent.

There was a skittering sound, as if little pebbles were bouncing along the skin of the capsule.

Then the heat pulse began.

Heat pulse was too weak a name. It was a fireball, engulfing the capsule, heat and light streaming past the window.

The capsule had become a comet, trailing a tail of fire as it hurtled toward Earth. And Kit was right in the middle of it.

But the interior wasn't hot. Not even warm. Which meant the heat shield should be holding.

He tried to look out the window to see if Texas was going by. But all he saw was the heat pulse, glowing orange. And bits of the heat shield flying by as they broke off. At least, he thought it was the heat shield. It was supposed to burn off in reentry, but was it burning off—or breaking up—too fast? He had no way to tell.

A bead of sweat dripped down his forehead and landed in the collar of his spacesuit. And he suddenly realized that it had become warm in the capsule. Almost unbearably so.

Did that mean the heat shield had come loose? He had no idea.

The capsule began to oscillate again and he checked his altitude. Time to deploy the drogue parachute. He hit the switch, and two seconds later the capsule jerked hard as the chute caught.

The oscillations stopped.

But the interior felt as if the temperature had gone up twenty degrees. His skin was slick with sweat, feeling as if it were blistering with the heat.

He was damned uncomfortable—but still alive. That was the thing to focus on.

Ten thousand feet. A massive jolt as the main parachute deployed, his seat restraints catching him hard and snapping his head back. Deceleration began in earnest, the pressure of it making it hard to swallow. And the heat. The capsule was turning into a sauna.

But his training held strong and he began to unhook what he could from his suit, preparing for a rapid egress if necessary. He was an aviator, and aviators didn't panic. Even when they were looking death in the eyes.

But the heat shield must have held—he'd made it this far.

Now all he had to do was survive the ocean landing. It would be a terrible thing to drown on his way back from the stars. He almost laughed at the thought as he wiped the sweat from his forehead, his eyes stinging.

The capsule hit the ocean with a splash, just as it had in training. But this time, the explosive bolts on the door held.

He wasn't going to drown. The heat shield had held. He was alive.

He was home.

He did laugh at the sheer fantasticalness of it all. He'd ridden a rocket, orbited Earth, and come back again. He and Anne-Marie would have a lot to talk about once he got back to Houston.

"Perseid Two, do you read? Perseid Two, do you read?"

The radio came back to life. Mission Control calling for him.

"Roger, I read you." He had to laugh again, because the situation was still so… beyond anything. He'd been to the stars. And now he was back. He was only the second American to ever do so. Only the fifth man in the entire history of human civilization to do so.

After that moment of mirth, he got back to work, flipping on the rescue beacon and going through his post-flight checklist.

"The destroyer is coming to get you," Parsons said. He didn't sound relieved. More like resigned, as if this success weighed on him.

Success made Kit feel light as a feather. As if he were still in zero G.

Kit heard the engines of the ship then, which seemed incredibly loud after the relative silence of his last twenty-four hours. The capsule swung as the hoist began to lift it, but it was more like the motion of a playground swing compared to the forces of the reentry. He felt as if he were on the world's slowest elevator. Then a *clunk* that rattled him inside the capsule.

The ship's deck. He was on the ship's deck. He heard cheering, faintly.

And then a knock at the hatch.

He released the bolts, shoved the door open, and stepped back onto Earth. Or at least onto a man-made surface.

The entire crew was on the deck and in formation, waiting for him. The captain came forward and snapped off a salute. "Commander Campbell, welcome home."

Kit returned the salute, then held out his hand. "Thank you, sir. It's good to be back."

And as soon as he could, he was going to find Anne-Marie and tell her that he was home for good.

A few hours later, they were out of deviled eggs. When Margie hung up from her check-up call she announced, "Well, he's coming back."

"Why?" Betty asked. "That's only been what, three orbits?"

"Is everything okay?" Anne-Marie asked. She'd kept the fear at bay successfully most of the day, but now it was creeping up again, clogging her throat.

"Bill wouldn't say why. Just that they've decided it's time for him to come back."

Anne-Marie wrapped her arms around her stomach. There wasn't any reason to be concerned. Everything was going well. Maybe they had enough data? Margie didn't seem worried. If she was going to do this— really try to be with Kit, to tell him she loved him, with everything that entailed—there would be other days like this. If not with him, then with Greg or Joe or Mitch.

"Well, good," she said at last. "I was thinking he'd been gone too long."

Frances laughed—a short, perfunctory bark—and slid her arm around Anne-Marie's back. On the television, a soap opera was droning on. Someone had amnesia. Or maybe it was a secret baby. They were in a hospital.

Anne-Marie's face was hot. Except where it was cold. And where it burned. Her skin was suddenly too tight on her hands. She wanted to itch and squirm. Except the only thing that could bring any relief was...

The phone rang. Margie answered, "Yes, Bill?" Several beats passed, and then she smiled. "They've got him."

Anne-Marie buried her face in Frances's neck for a minute. They had him. He was back. He was safe.

Margie kept talking, and Betty was clapping. Frances suggested opening some champagne. Anne-Marie just focused on the air moving in and out of her lungs.

He was coming home. He'd survived. Now they had to make things right.

CHAPTER TWENTY

The evening after his successful, historic orbit—and those were just a few of the words from the headlines—Anne-Marie could tell when Kit's car arrived in the neighborhood. It might have been the honking. Or the cheering. Or maybe that Margie had called her when he left ASD with an estimate of his arrival time. Come to think, J. Edgar Hoover could probably save himself a lot of hassle by just putting Margie on the payroll.

Freddie and Lisa were sitting in the front room, looking out the window for him.

"He's here!" Lisa shouted.

"Give him a second to get out of the car," Anne-Marie called back.

She finished setting the table. She'd made beef Wellington, and those potatoes au gratin he liked, and a new creamed spinach recipe Margie had clipped from a catalog for her. And two kinds of pies, because she wasn't sure if he preferred apple or chocolate chess. It was too much food—much too much—but she hadn't known what else to do with all the energy zinging through her body. It was either cook or lift the house clean off its foundation. She'd gone with the food.

She was straightening the napkins for the third time when a quiet knock came at the back door.

"It's Kit!" Freddie shouted. He bolted for it with Lisa at his heels.

Anne-Marie stayed in the dining room, fussing with her dress. She'd gone with purple—against the wishes of both Betty and Margie. It seemed more space-aged.

A moment later, Kit came into the dining room, a child dangling off each hand and Bucky running around them, barking.

Kit looked good. His chin boasted a layer of scruff. His clothes were wrinkled. But he was beautiful. And when he smiled at her, all eye-crinkles and joy, she knew he was hers.

"Hi," she said—because she was incredibly articulate. When he didn't say anything in response, she added, "You're back."

"I am. I, uh, got your note." He pulled a crumpled piece of legal paper out of his pocket. She'd left it on his kitchen counter.

It wasn't anything elaborate or particularly romantic: *Please come for dinner. A-M Smith.* She'd signed it because she didn't think he'd know her handwriting, which was probably a sign she shouldn't tell him she loved him. But she'd decided she was sort of a risk-taker. And besides, it was the truth.

"I haven't changed or showered or anything," Kit said. "I'm sorry."

The words were offered with gut-deep conviction and applied to everything. A man who could apologize, hmm? Well, she'd take it.

"You're forgiven. This time."

He smiled back at her—not practiced and charming. Not the smile everyone else got. But a private, intimate, happy grin.

And on seeing it, and knowing that he understood her, it took every ounce of self-control Anne-Marie possessed not to throw herself at him. But the children were there and the man needed to eat. So she reached for her napkin and batted at her eyes.

Clearing her throat, she said, "Kids, give the man some room and take your seats. I, uh, made beef Wellington. For some reason, I couldn't get a turkey."

Kit took a step toward her until he filled her vision. Until she could smell him and feel his heat and almost taste him. "There is nothing in the Milky Way like your cooking. I made sure."

He didn't touch her, but he didn't need to. They were fine, or they were going to be. Confessing that she loved him wouldn't be easy, knowing when and how to tell the kids would be harder, dealing with the press would be awful, but Kit would always be there to catch her.

"You didn't like space food?"

He laughed, and then sobered. "No, it turns out everything I want is right here."

She took his plate and piled it high with food. She set it down in his place. "Good."

The next twenty minutes were a crush of questions from Freddie and Lisa. Kit told them about seeing stars in the middle of the day, of the lights he could see on Earth from up above. He described how from space, the earth was blue and beautiful.

Then Lisa turned to Anne-Marie. "Beau West pushed me during recess."

"He what?"

"He pushed me. And I told Mrs. Green and Beau got detention."

"But did he apologize?" Kit asked, concern in his eyes.

"Yes, but I don't think he seemed very sorry."

Not to be outdone, Freddie said, "Robbie Reynolds saw a coral snake down by the lake."

"Tell me how he knew it was a coral snake," Kit asked.

"The red and yellow stripes were next to each other."

"Red touches yellow kills a fellow," Kit and Freddie said together.

And at that, Anne-Marie had to laugh. Because the most famous man in America was sitting at their table, and the kids wanted to talk about playground fights and snakes. And he wanted them to.

She laughed until her shoulders were quivering, until she had to wipe her eyes with her napkin and take a few deep breaths to settle down. She really owed her parents another thank you for the house. Who could have predicted it would come with one ideal next-door neighbor?

"You okay?" Kit asked, smiling.

"Perfect."

And she was.

Anne-Marie handed the last plate to Kit, which he carefully dried before setting it into the cupboard.

It had been an uneventful meal. The kids had asked about the flight, but once he'd described the lift off and weightlessness and told them that he hadn't seen any aliens or even Mars, they'd wanted to talk about school and their friends. Which was fine with him. After typing up his report and talking to the press, he was a little tired of discussing the flight.

The kids were asleep, the dishes were done, Bucky was fed... one last thing for him to do tonight. The most important thing.

Anne-Marie set her hip against the counter and gave him a look. One that asked, *What's next?*

He knew what he wanted next. He only hoped she wanted it too.

He caught her hand. "Come look at the stars with me."

They slipped through the back door, hand in hand, shutting the slider as quietly as possible to keep from waking the kids.

It felt very… married.

Before he'd met her, such a feeling would have sent him into a panic. But now it felt right. Perfect. He wanted this feeling every night, sharing it with this woman.

Once they were outside, she threw herself into his arms and he caught her gladly. He kissed her hard under the stars, pouring all of his longing and relief into it. *Finally, I'm home.*

The kiss had heat, but wasn't scorching. It was a prelude to the rest of their lives.

After a time, he pulled away. As enjoyable as this was, he had some things to say. "I'm sorry I called you a distraction. You're not. Well, you are. But the best kind."

She set a hand on his chest. "The wives—they explained things to me. How it was about more than my feelings. Or even yours."

He couldn't lie about that. "It *was* about more than us. I never would have hurt you for anything less. But now that it's over…" God, he hoped he was doing this right. He couldn't read the expression on her face, had to forge ahead blindly. "It could be about just us from now on. And the kids. If you wanted."

That was it. He only hoped it would be enough for her.

Her posture seemed considering but not yielding—for all that she stayed in his arms. "You'll still be an astronaut," she pointed out. Which wasn't an answer.

He'd always be an astronaut—he'd grabbed a record that no one else could touch now. But there would be others going to space behind him. "The press won't care so much about me once the preparations for the next mission start." At least, he hoped they wouldn't.

"It's not the press I'm worried about. It's us."

His heart sank. His life, the scrutiny he was under—it was too much.

"When you were up there," she went on, "I was never so scared in my life. No one has ever made me feel so much, not even Doug. The kids, of course, but that's different. Kit, I was terrified."

"I'm not going up again. Once was enough." And it was. A man couldn't live up in the stars.

Kit wanted to make his life with her.

She eased against him, sighing. "What was it like?" Her words floated in wonder.

"The stars were... they were pretty." Once again, words failed him. "The best part was the weightlessness, really. It's like you're swimming through air, all of you buoyant and free. I wouldn't mind that again." He rubbed his mouth against her hair, breathed deeply of her scent. "Actually, the best part was seeing Earth. It was perfect. Like heaven floating there in space. And knowing that you and the kids were down there, safe and sound, waiting for me to come back..." He swallowed hard. "That was the best part," he admitted huskily.

"You coming back safely was the best part," she said.

His chest tightened. Her confession gave him hope enough to ask his ultimate question. "I had some time to think, waiting for the launch, and I was wondering if maybe you'd let me court you."

He held himself still, waiting, hoping. He'd survived a trip to space; he could survive a rejection from her. Couldn't he?

She looked up at him, but said nothing, her expression rather like a judge's, weighing what he'd said in her mind. Perhaps a woman who'd been burned before in marriage couldn't be tempted into it again.

"Or not," he went on. "We could go on being neighbors. Neighbors having a secret affair." Not really what he wanted, but he'd take what he could get from her. "But I should warn you: your kids are really smart. They'll figure out something's up sooner or later."

Maybe a low blow to use the kids, but he was getting desperate.

She gave a small laugh. "Are you trying to chase away my other suitors, Commander Campbell?"

"You bet I am. Because I love you."

A small smile played over her mouth. It wasn't cold or sarcastic or removed.

"That's convenient. Because it so happens that I love you too."

"Everything is going my way, then." He tightened his arms around her, attempting to pull her in to seal it with a kiss.

Anne-Marie, however, had other ideas. She put her hand over his mouth. "You know that Doug... that is, he wasn't faithful to me. At all. I won't put up with that again."

"You won't have to. Since I met you, I haven't been able to think of another woman."

"All Houston's blondes will be so sad."

"I prefer redheads." She made a face. "I prefer you." She rolled her eyes, but then she preened like a satisfied cat. "So is it true, Mrs. Smith? Are you mine?"

Her smile was wide, brighter than even the sun at noon, and his heart leapt. "Well, I'm certainly not anyone else's."

He kissed her then with the stars as witness. They could gape all they liked. The only things he was interested in now were earthbound.

EPILOGUE

Cape Canaveral, Florida
Three Months Later

"**O**h my goodness, we're going to see an actual launch! Up close!" Lisa practically sang out that last bit as she climbed out of the car, pushing past her brother in her haste to get closer to the launch site.

"Hang on," Kit called. "And we're not getting that close. Just closer than most people." He shook his head as Lisa ignored him.

Both the kids had been over the moon when he'd told them he was taking them to see the next launch. Almost as excited as they'd been when Anne-Marie had announced that she was going to marry him. Today the kids' excitement level had shot outside the solar system.

He didn't blame them. He'd learned a few things about excitement and shock over the past few months. He kept waiting for Anne-Marie to change her mind or realize he was getting the better end of the deal. She hadn't, though. She just kept making him pot roast and rolling her eyes at him. But she also let him kiss her, so the heady feeling kept going. It was better than lift off.

Freddie hopped alongside his sister, the both of them vibrating out of their skin. Anne-Marie came along behind, looking less impressed than her children.

Kit held back by the car, just watching them as they walked toward the rocket. His family. Or soon to be, at any rate.

Anne-Marie stopped, turned back to him. "Aren't you coming? We can't get in without you."

This might be his favorite view of her. The gingham dress showed off her trim waist and the flare of her hips. And the saucy look she was giving him? He hoped he never got over the jolt she gave him. ASD could keep the rockets; he'd found what he needed in her.

"Yep."

They went past security and found their way to where the more minor dignitaries were: other astronauts, a couple of the more senior engineers.

Freddie and Lisa said hello to the astronauts with slightly less awe than they had the first time at Margie's dinner party. They were already getting used to this space life.

Then the kids moved on to the engineers and questioned them about every aspect of the launch, including some things Kit himself didn't know or care about. They really were such smart kids. They were going to go far.

He himself hung back, holding onto Anne-Marie's left hand, the one wearing the simple engagement ring they'd picked out together. She was craning her neck to peer up to the top of the rocket, her mouth slightly open. She looked adorable.

"You rode at the top of one of those?" she asked under her breath.

"I did." Truth be told, he was feeling a little overwhelmed looking at the rocket from here. He had ridden a rocket to space? And had come back again?

He'd done it, and it still felt a little unreal.

"It's so big," she said, softly, awestruck.

Mine was bigger. Or maybe, *I never get tired of hearing you say that.* He looked around for Carruthers, who'd probably offer, "That's what all the girls tell me," but Kit held back. This was a historic occasion, after all.

The five-minute countdown started over the loudspeaker and everyone settled into place. The kids came back. Lisa stood in front of her mother so Anne-Marie could loosely hug her from behind. Freddie took a place next to Kit. Kit put a hand on his shoulder, thinking that Freddie would be embarrassed by a hug. Or at least Kit would've been at his age.

They all watched the waiting rocket, quiet. Antici-
pating.

Finally, finally: "Ten, nine, eight…"

Kit held his breath too as "Ignition!" rang out from
the speakers.

The ground beneath their feet began to vibrate,
clouds billowing from the bottom of the rocket. Kit
tightened his hold on Freddie's shoulder.

The rocket lifted from the ground sluggishly. That
had surprised Kit at first, how languid the launch really
was.

Anne-Marie's and the kids' mouths dropped open,
their expressions now ones of open wonder. Kit just
watched them all, enjoying their reactions. He'd seen a
rocket launch before, but their reactions were infinitely
more enjoyable.

The rocket finally slipped free of its mooring, the
tower falling away, and made its escape from the atmosphere.

They all watched in silence until the rocket disappeared into the blue.

As soon as it did the kids started bouncing again.
"Oh my…" Freddie snuck a glance at his mom.
"Gosh," he finished lamely.

Kit laughed, because he understood the impulse.
Gosh didn't quite cover a rocket launch, but Anne-

Marie had surprisingly strong feelings about profanity. It was good he was coming into Freddie's life.

"When will he be back?" Lisa asked.

"Two days," Kit said.

"I hope he comes back safely," Anne-Marie said, giving Kit a look that was half worried, half appreciative.

"They'll bring him back just fine," Kit said, returning her look. "Like they did with me."

He'd seen the stars, he'd felt weightless, he'd made history. But that was over. He'd given the public their share. He was keeping the rest for himself—and for her.

He clapped his hands to get the kids' attention. "Okay. What should we do today? Go to the beach?"

"The beach, the beach!" the kids yelled.

"Commander Campbell," a reporter called at him, "can we get a statement about…"

Kit waved his hand. "No, I'm sorry. I'm not Commander Campbell today. I'm just here for the launch."

"He never stops being Commander Campbell." That was Anne-Marie, who squeezed his waist and beamed at the reporter. "He'll answer a question or two, and we can even pose for a picture if you like."

Later, Kit wasn't sure if he'd answered the question. He didn't remember it, at any rate. What he remembered was Anne-Marie getting her kids and Margie's lined up for the cameraman. The sweet sweep of her neck as she bent to laugh at something Robbie Reynolds said. The way she fit perfectly under his arm.

She was perfect.

Once the pictures were over, one of the reporters started to ask something else, but he placed a firm hand on Anne-Marie and Lisa and began towing them away, Freddie trailing behind. "We've had enough, gentlemen. Now I'm going to the beach with my family."

AFTERWORD

There are similarities between the plot of *Star Dust*
and the actual history of human space exploration. The
first human to orbit the earth was Soviet cosmonaut
Yuri Gagarin in April 1961. American John Glenn
followed in February 1962. However, the American
Space Department is fictional. ASD is not NASA; the
Perseid mission is not Mercury. All the characters in
Star Dust are literary inventions and any resemblance
to persons living or dead is coincidental.

Two incidents in the book closely track history.
First, during a test in 1961, Gus Grissom nearly
drowned after the bolts on a hatch blew early and the
capsule filled with water. Second, in the process of
John Glenn's 1962 orbit, there were questions about
whether the heat shield was in place; later it was de-
termined to have been a faulty switch, not a mechani-
cal failure.

In addition to inventing an entire cast of characters,
we have changed a number of historical details. For
example, all the astronauts chosen for the Mercury,
Gemini, and Apollo programs were married—
probably to avoid the kinds of distractions Kit faces

301

here. In the early and mid 1960s, the astronauts and their wives attempted to project happiness and stability even when the truth about their marriages was more complicated.

Public scrutiny of the astronauts and their families *was* intense. A divorcee like Anne-Marie might have faced severe backlash for her involvement with an astronaut. If anything, we've underplayed the media's interest and involvement in this novel. We've also eschewed references to the financial incentives the astronauts' families received for participating in the media coverage about their lives.

The neighborhood where Kit and Anne-Marie live—Lake Glade—is inspired by Timber Cove and Clear Lake, Houston subdivisions located near the Manned Spacecraft Center (later Johnson Space Center) where many astronauts and NASA employees lived.

We are grateful to a number of authors of histories of space exploration and NASA, including Tom Wolfe, Lily Koppel, Francis French, Colin Burgess, and Martha Ackmann, and for the NASA Oral History Project, which is entertaining and informative. We have also enjoyed atmospheric fiction written in the 1950s and 1960s, including that by Sloan Wilson, John Cheever, and Mary McCarthy and films from the period, including *Lover Come Back*, *Pillow Talk*, and

The Apartment. We're going to keep making stuff up, but these books and movies have given us parameters.

ACKNOWLEDGEMENTS

This is a book about hope and risk and potential. As such, its writing and editing required group effort.

Star Dust would not exist without the support of our friends and family. You always understood when we need to hide away to scribble "our stories," your antics helped us write children (and dogs!) with verisimilitude, and you gladly ate 60s food and drank 60s cocktails "for research." We love you.

We must also thank our beta readers: Elisabeth Lane and Erin Satie who read an early (weak) draft; Kimberly Truesdale, Molly O'Keefe, and Soni Wolf who helped us through the middle; and Cecilia Grant, Melody, and Cindy who helped us polish at the end. You corrected errors and cheered us on even when we had miles to go.

Star Dust would have been immeasurably weaker without the editing of Simone St. James. Any remaining errors are ours.

A fuller list of the things we read and watched in order to write *Star Dust* appears in the authors' note, but we are grateful to the brave men and women who participated in early human space exploration. Whatever this book is, you inspired it.

ABOUT THE AUTHORS

Emma Barry is a novelist, full-time mama, and recovering academic. When she's not reading or writing, she loves hugs from her preschooler twins, her husband's cooking, her cat's whiskers, her dog's tail, and Earl Grey tea.

You can find her on the web at
www.authoremmabarry.com.

Genevieve Turner writes romance fresh from the Golden State. In a previous life, she was a scientist studying the genetics of behavior, but now she's a stay at home mom studying the intersection of nature and nurture in her own kids. (So far, nature is winning!) She lives in beautiful Southern California, where she manages her family and homestead in an indolent manner.

You can find her on the web at www.genturner.com.

Manufactured by Amazon.com
Columbia, SC
30 March 2017